DIRTY
OLD
WOMEN

*Erotica by women of
experience*

Edited by
Lynx Canon

Cover design by Mike 064 Freeman. Published by Tale of the Lynx.

TABLE OF CONTENTS

INTRODUCTION

In 2014, I started writing a memoir about my sexual history, which has been brave, complicated, varied, and always interesting. It seemed risky. I wanted to write honestly about the sex I've had, but wondered how people would react to a woman in her sixties talking about sex. After all, older women are so often ridiculed for daring to step out of the stereotypes, for daring to claim our still-lively lust.

Then I met another woman – in her 70s, even more ancient than me – who'd just published her own sexual memoir. Maybe this was a thing? Maybe there were a lot of us who were looking back on our younger selves with wise eyes and who were eager to tell stories of our wild pasts and our sometimes wilder present.

I decided to find out.

Oakland's Octopus Literary Salon was just opening in a new space in the buzzy Uptown district. Co-owners Rebecca Grove and Ian Patton wanted to make the café a community resource with a full schedule of arts, literary and music events with the help of events director Mike Linn. They warmly welcomed my idea for a monthly erotica reading series.

I called the series Dirty Old Women, taking the pejorative and giving it a proud spin.

It turns out that there are plenty of hot and talented older women in the San Francisco Bay Area and they were burning to have a place to come together (pun gleefully intended).

Another surprise was that there are plenty of other folks – not necessarily old or female – who wanted to hear us read sexy fiction and poems. It didn't hurt that the women who read at the Octopus are amazing performers who turn their readings into erotic theater.

That's certainly part of the reason we've had standing-room-only crowds this year. Another reason, I think, is that everyone is hungry for an authentic conversation about desire, sex and intimacy. We dirty old women tend to write about real sex between real people, with all the confusion, fear, excitement and yearning that accompanies the real thing.

I also hope that when we stand up there, with our wrinkles, gray hair and unabashed desire, we reassure young women that it's not over at thirty, or fifty or even ninety.

Every one of us deserves to be able to speak our desires and demand pleasure. And you deserve to read these stories of unabashed desire and intense pleasure, written in a delightful variety of flavors.

XO Lynx

Selene Steese, author of the collection *Woman Growing Wings*, says writing saved her life. "I felt very lonely growing up. Words gave me focus, provided a lens through which I could make sense of the world. I can't imagine a healthier or more life-affirming addiction than my obsession with committing poetry." She began writing spicy poetry ten years ago and credits the practice with losing eighty pounds, recovering her vitality and rediscovering her yoni. As this poem makes clear, she's discovered plenty.

Selene Steese

ALL I WANT TO DO IS GET OFF

At night when I'm watching TV
I wonder what it would be like
to have every man I see
down on his knees
in front of me,
teasing my panties
down past my knees.

As I stand at the sink
trying to concentrate on making
dinner, my nether mouth
is throbbing in my pants,
cooking itself
in its own juices.

While I'm chopping zucchini
for a stir fry,
all I want to do
is take a stiff one
up my cunt.

All I want to do is get off,
and on the subject of getting off,

I only know how to be blunt.

This ain't perimenopause
or menopause or
any kind of pause—
it's just full speed ahead, and damn,
there had better be torpedoes!

Everything is foreplay:
The weight of my dress
against my skin, soft cloth
perched across my nipples.

The slippery texture
of a perfectly cooked
piece of zucchini
as it slides down my throat.

The smooth, hard, hot surface
of the cup that holds
my morning tea

All I can think about is sex.

I've heard that men think about sex
every few seconds.

Hell, I don't think about sex.
I AM sex!

I am the embodiment of humping,
screwing, shagging, and fucking
and it doesn't seem to matter
how often I do it—

The more often I do, the more often
I want to do it.

Bring on any man, anywhere, anytime
and I will wear him out!

I want to come and come and come
and come until my nether mouth
starts to shout!

I refuse to stop until I hear the word
"Enough" directly from my other
set of lips!

Until then, I am going to be slotting
Duracell long-lifes into my vibrator
saddling up that lone silicone ranger
and rocking my womanly hips!

Kristin McCloy was a bona fide *enfant terrible*. She made waves when she was just 26 with the 1989 Random House publication of *Velocity,* a novel *People Magazine* called a sex-propelled meditation on death and bikers. She followed that up with two more novels, *Some Girls* (1994) and *Hollywood Savages* (2010). Lucky for us, while birthing her fourth novel, she's also playing with full-on erotica that still retains a gorgeous sense of place and time, in this case, one golden evening in San Francisco.

EVENING IN SAN FRANCISCO

She felt like she'd always lived in the Haight. She'd been twenty-three years old when she got there, and twenty-nine years later, she was still there, and back in love with it, especially on rainy nights like tonight, when new city people were kept indoors by the weather while she and the other intrepids wandered out to find it not cold but in fact balmy: a mid-October evening where the cars swished down newly washed streets like small waves, and the prismatic red and yellow and green and amber and deep blue lights were refracted everywhere up from the sidewalk, making of the streets a kind of wonderland, the rainbows making her feel at once revealed, mysterious and blonder.

She was average height, somewhat less in weight, with broad shoulders, a woman who still wore the clothes of her youth, because she'd never stopped, only added to her repertoire (which also included Mature Woman, Holy Sweat-Suited Woman and Older-but- STILL-Younger-than-Thou-and-Baby, I-Could-Be-Your- Mama.)

Tonight it was her favorite fifteen-year-old Levis, happily tight on her ass (thank you San Francisco, she liked to think when she was huffing up the steeper streets), paired with a sparkly black shirt left loose, her ancient, long-faded red Doc Martins and an Army/Navy surplus jacket.

She had good legs, breasts that rode high, a decent ass, soft abs. She wasn't classically beautiful but her face had character and her eyes were a startling grey, the irises outlined in an inkier tone, with their dark pupils suggesting depths.

She had never had a problem finding lovers and she'd had some good runs. Eleven passionate years with R until their interests drifted and their lust faded. And the urbane G, who knew every hot spot before it even opened but who, despite some truly hot sex, had decided to choose the gay side of bi.

In between men, she hung out with a cabal of like-minded women now long, long friends, as well as her younger colleagues in the IT department of a media company, a job that was three parts tedium to two parts engrossing, which she figured was as good odds as she was ever going to get.

She was happy with her life, happy with her two companions, Ace and Zelly, both gorgeous independent creatures who nevertheless slept on her bed every night, their perfect feline faces and Luna-moth eyes the last and first things she saw every evening and each morning.

But tonight, she couldn't stay in. She was sick of herbal tea and Amazon Prime. In truth, she'd consumed half a bottle of Ménage à Trois red, had popcorn with garlic salt and nutritional yeast for dinner, and binged on her favorite series, telling herself she'd quit after each episode then letting the next one begin until it was all over, which inevitably left her with a hollow sadness – and tonight, an added load of restlessness.

She wanted company, she craved conversation; she was sick and tired of being alone. And the best thing about San Francisco – or at any rate, the best thing about the Haight – was that she didn't have to be.

She lived a five-minute walk away from her favorite bar, the Gold Idle, a spacious place with a round table in the window, a fabulous jukebox, a beautiful little patio in the back where in fine weather people bunched up on the stairs, smoked and talked talked talked. But tonight she didn't want to chat with them; that wasn't the comfort she was seeking.

She went to the juke and put on Norah Jones' Come Away with Me, Tracey Thorne singing with Massive Attack, several tracks of Thelonious Monk Alone in San Francisco, and Stan Getz playing with Astrud and Jobim. It was the perfect music for a drizzling, slightly tropical night.

She found a stool at the bar in between a couple of young people she'd never seen before – they weren't together, she didn't think –, and ordered a vodka martini. "Dirty, but not a total slut," which garnered a grin from each of her neighbors and Max the bartender. He was a good sport. He'd heard the line before, but always smiled at her as if it were the first time.

"I like that," said the young woman on her right, a zaftig blonde with a beautiful heart-shaped face and big blue eyes, and, like an echo, the young guy on her left said, "I'ma steal that."

He was some type of biracial, the type that got the best of both worlds. His eyes were slightly almond, chocolate brown, his skin olive, his body lean, and he was growing himself some dreads that framed his face beautifully.

Luce was charmed. Young people did that to her, with their ardent cynicism not quite belying the idealists within, their eco-seriousness (which she shared, oh by *all* means), their huge hopes and wild dreams, their paltry daytime jobs, their taut skin and shiny smiles.

And these two were almost too cute for words. Especially the young man, whose type she and her friends called "angel boys." They tended toward delicate necklaces and thumb rings, had Sanskrit tattoos on their wing blades, wore their hair long and were perennially clad in skinny black jeans and Converse sneakers, thrift-store handyman shirts and jackets (a lot like the one she was wearing, if much bigger); boys who rode bikes or skateboards everywhere, with messenger bags slung across their backs. They almost always had sweet, long-lashed eyes and beautiful mouths. They loved their mothers, adored their sisters and weren't scared to hug each other long and hard, to pull apart and grin then hug again.

"I'm Luce, by the way," she said, glancing at first one then the other.

"Amanda," said the blonde girl, the word shy in her mouth.

"Iggy," said the boy, and as Luce smiled, he rolled his eyes, smiling back; his teeth were perfect. "Yeah," he said, "My mom's a big fan."

His mother, she thought. How much younger or older might she be than Luce herself?

The bar was empty enough for Luce to pull her stool slightly back and, by natural extension, for the other two to pull theirs slightly in, the three of them leaning forward in tacit compliance so that they made a kind of circle.

Luce asked after them. What did they do (temped, bar-backed) –

"No," she interrupted, she meant in their "Real Lives?"

"I write poetry," Amanda said, and Iggy confessed he was a musician. He could play guitar, bass, and even drums – in a pinch, he added.

"How wonderful!" Luce said truthfully, though she would have guessed as much. Artistic young people scraping by in San Francisco were *de rigueur*, and the best part was how this created a commonality, gave them something they all loved to talk about: music, and lyrics, Leonard Cohen, Anne Sexton –

"What a name!'" said Iggy lasciviously. Could he be directing that at Luce? Surely not?

Meanwhile, it seemed as though Amanda's chair had drifted closer. Yes, it had to have, because now she could feel Amanda's sweet, round thigh against her own, and Luce found herself staring at Iggy's hands, idle on the bar – the beautiful articulated hands of a musician, lingering very near Luce's own.

They were drinking shots. Tequila, Iggy had insisted, and when Luce said, "Well then, it's Patron," she saw the quick, frightened look the other two exchanged.

"I'm paying," Luce said sternly, knowing how much of their weekly paychecks these drinks cost, and though they'd demurred, it hadn't taken much for them to give in.

The talk grew looser, more personal. Where they'd grown up, what they loved best about the city, whether they were in love.

"Sorta," Amanda said, lowering her lashes, "But this person doesn't know I exist."

"Not me, not anymore," Iggy said, half rueful, half relieved.

"What about you?" he'd asked then. "I know you got someone at home!"

"I do," Luce said soberly, just to see if his face fell (it did, a little, and she hated herself, a little, for the swift leap of happiness it gave her). "My kitties, Zelly and Ace."

"Noooo," Iggy said, eyes dancing again.

"*Really?*" Amanda asked, that shy smile flashing past.

"Jesus," Luce thought. "What the hell is going on here?"

"You guys smoke?" Iggy asked, in a voice that didn't need any more lowering, but it made him sound just a little bit bad, and he bent his face so his baby dreads fell forward to hide it.

"I do," Amanda said.

"Let's see...last time I smoked was...hmmm....last night," Luce confirmed, and smiled when she saw them look at each other, another quick glance, this one of pure delight.

"Let's go out for a minute then," Iggy said.

They stood under the umbrella in the lightly misted air and partook of the raggediest joint Luce had seen in a long, long time.

Still, it was strong enough that after they went back to the bar, she turned to them impulsively and said, "Listen, you two. It's still early, and I have Patron and some purple Kush at home. I live just a few blocks from here, near Clayton. Wanna go there instead of spending all our money here?"

"Yes!" Iggy said, his grin huge, already grabbing his jacket. Amanda nodded, somehow even shyer now, her smile very sweet, and picked up her London Fog trench coat. It went wonderfully with her beautiful patent-leather pumps, and striding between the two of them, Luce reached out with sudden confidence and grabbed their hands, Amanda's tiny and boneless, Iggy's strong, his fingers instantly intertwining hers.

They walked down the street like that, impeding the few other pedestrians, grinning like little kids, their hands swinging between them, lights refracting. Luce could feel the night's mist clinging to her eyelashes, and she blinked so that she would feel it on her cheeks, too, downy and so so soft.

"'Not even the rain,'" Luce quoted, turning to Amanda, who finished, "'has such small hands.'"

Iggy said, "E.e. cummings," surprising them both, and making of them sudden and close conspirators.

Back at her place, the cats fled beneath the sofa to watch the strangers from a safe place, green eyes blinking, and Luce went about choosing music, lighting candles, putting a bottle of Patron and three beautiful tall shot glasses from her freezer on the table, before pulling out the little cedar box where she kept her weed and her new, pretty little vape.

She sat on the couch, and Iggy draped himself next to her, while Amanda chose a big floor pillow and sat at her feet, her eyes luminous, her skin so perfect it seemed to be emitting light.

Luce kept having to suppress a desire to burst out laughing, and then the desire to text her friends Josette, Audrey and Kathryn ("I think I'm about to have a three-way!" she wanted to write scandalously, imagining each of them already in bed by now, listening to the radio and reading novels, or just playing Words with Friends and besting each other).

They had another shot of Patron.

"A healthy shot," Luce said, pouring, "none of that anemic shit bartenders give you."

Everybody giggled, but nobody talked. After a few seconds, Iggy leaned in closer.

"I wanted to know," he said (oh, that husky angel voice!) "Would it be okay if I kissed you?"

"Who?" Luce said startled.

"Both of you," he answered, and before she could say anything else one hand was gentle on the back of her neck, so big that his fingers curved around to her throat, and his soft lips were on hers, asking nothing, just gently pressing. She opened her mouth and their tongues touched, but only barely.

With his free hand, Iggy reached down and next thing there was Amanda, smelling of peaches and summer grass, her impossibly soft skin against both their faces, and their mouths were turning, toward one then the other, like sunflowers toward the light, the kisses as soft as the rain that had begun again and was pattering against the skylight, playing a duet with Coltrane's Gentle Side.

"Can we...?" Amanda surprised her by asking, nodding toward the weed, and Luce said, "Of course!"

She loaded a hit for each of them, and the second she'd released a big plume of white smoke, Iggy took the vape from her hand and pulled both of them back into the kissing circle, the herbal taste a kind of perfumed bitterness...until suddenly Luce found herself in her head, every bit of sensuality usurped by her brain, nervous chatter like a loop:

whatamIdoing/whoarethesepeople/whyareweatmy house/I'mmuchtoo old old old old forthisstuff/forthesekids/ can'ttheyseethelinesaroundmyeyes/ LAUGHLINESBEPROUDSTUPIDWOMAN!/ohJesusI-thinktheygottago/ whatdoI/howdoI/whydidI

– until both the others had pulled back to look at her, such concern in their faces, Amanda's small hand reaching to stroke the tendrils of Luce's hair away from her face, while Iggy simply leaned back, giving her space.

"Are you okay?" Amanda asked.

Iggy quietly poured them all another shot, then went to the kitchen and filled a glass with filtered water, brought it back and knelt before her, holding it up as an offering.

He was mute, but his eyes said everything. The vulnerability there, the calm courage of it, suddenly let her out of her head and back into the room with these two beautiful beings.

She reached out and felt her soul flow back into the tips of her fingers, into her lips, it seemed even into her eyelashes, a kind of purr that made her aware of her body, of the thrumming that had started between her legs, of the way her breath had sped up when she saw one side of Iggy's black jeans begin to grow.

"Nothing," she said. "Nothing is wrong. Nothing nothing nothing. You are my angels. You are welcome in my home."

Amanda laughed and then she hugged one of Luce's legs, one hand sweetly stroking up her inner thigh, sighing against her as if she had just heard that nobody was hurt, that everything was going to be okay, everything was going to be just fine fine *fine*.

Which made Luce giggle, and then all three of them were laughing, leaning into each other, laughing precisely at the same un-nameable thing, which made them laugh harder. Then Amanda snorted and that made them laugh even more.

Iggy started putting his hands into the women's hair, he pulled them close, and then again they were kissing, kissing, kissing, kissing, kissing and it was like language, each of them pouring themselves out, letting themselves be seen, their eyes soft, heavy-lidded, everybody's hands roving now, moving softly up his shirt to Iggy's strong chest, his firm biceps, and Amanda's mounded breasts, she reaching back to unclasp herself, then leaning forward to pull at Luce's zipper –

"WAIT."

Everything stopped.

"Is – did I do something wrong?" Amanda asked. Her face flushed hot.

"No, no, no, it's not that – just – please wait, okay? Oh, and let's –" Luce picked up her shot and the others followed suit. She threw it back without a toast, tried for a confident smile and nearly flew out of the room.

Where the *fuck* was her coconut oil –

Oh yeah with her vibrator (that thing had cost her a chunk, and she'd barely used it – she needed her mind more than vibration to make her clit come alive again – well, not *again* it wasn't quite that, it was more like alive the way it used to feel, when even a nearby breath could make it tingle).

"Broken pussy," she muttered, a line from a TV rap song that had made her laugh really hard, and just then she found it, her little jar full of the thick white paste that reminded her of her mother's Crisco (Crisco! She thought. Jesus, the things we ate – God they were good) – but smelled like the islands, like great tropical drinks and amazing Jamaican shrimp.

She peeled her jeans off and squatted unceremoniously, then took her small red spatula and spooned the stuff up inside, feeling the oil glistening against her thumbs, so she rubbed it into her still-downy hair (God she was so glad she'd never shaved there THANK YOU MOM) and into the hollows of her thighs, still good thighs, strong, with a nice concavity and curve of flank.

About to put her jeans back on, instead she found one of her father's elegant French-cuffed white shirts and tossed it over her pretty pink lace bra, then found a thong that matched and put it on, too.

"I'm not dead, I'm coming," she half-yelled, and everybody started laughing again. Oh, the promise of that unintended sentence, she thought, if only, *please* God, Goddess, it's time!

She did a funny sashay into the room, and the other two laughed at her and instantly began shedding their own clothes. Iggy pulled his jeans off to reveal something near-to-scary tenting his boxer briefs, and Amanda, her thin silk vest already doffed, shimmied out of her long flowing skirt so that she was left (braless, apparently) in a silky shirt. She did, Luce notice, retain her extremely sexy black pumps with ankle straps, and she saw now that this was because Amanda had perfect ankles, strong and delicate, like the stalks of a flower holding up the very bottom of the bloom.

She was also wearing some of the most delicate lingerie Luce had ever seen. She came to kneel next to Amanda, pulling at the cushions everywhere to create a pile, sticking them in the middle, and gratefully Iggy came down to join them, watching as Luce lightly touched the hem of Amanda's pearl gray silky slip, with tiny little pearl button insets, and Belgian lace laying across thighs plump and absolutely free of cellulite.

"This is so beautiful. Do you always wear this kind of thing when you go out?" Luce asked softly.

"Only when I want to feel sexy," Amanda said. "Sometimes it doesn't matter if anybody else sees you that way, as long as you do."

Iggy cupped Amanda's face and kissed her, very sweetly, with a lot of tongue. It was a reward, this was clear, for the way she thought.

Oh my god these people, Luce thought, these *young* people!

And then Amanda was unbuttoning the shirt Luce had just buttoned up, and Iggy came to sit behind her, his legs around her so that his thighs fit, hard and hairy against the backs of her own, putting his mouth against her neck and letting Amanda place his hands on Luce's breasts, cupping them like a fruit-buyer testing for weight, and making low, long mmmm's of satisfaction.

Amanda – suddenly so competent, so in charge! – then propped another cushion under Luce's ass, and put one under her own knees so that she was on all fours before coming down on her elbows but keeping her knees bent, so that her own ass (as heart-shaped as her face!) swayed high, the slip slipping (as slips surely were meant to do) up a back that could compete in shapeliness with the prettiest of cellos, and Luce had to reach out and touch that porcelain skin, running just the tips of her fingers along Amanda's body, feeling the goosebumps rise, before becoming immediately distracted by the younger woman's tongue against her thong, wetting that small strip, kissing her clit through the cloth which somehow was more electrifying than having it kissed directly, and Luce moaned, she arched her back, making a small space beneath her which Iggy scooted into, and she could feel his cock now, she reached for it, thick and hard and silky all at once, the throb of his heartbeat something she could feel beneath her palm. She closed her fist around it tightly (it just barely fit) and heard him moan in her ear.

Amanda pulled Luce's thong off with the same surprising deftness, and Iggy lifted her hips and placed her so that the tip of his cock was now entering her coconut oil-slicked pussy, making her eyes widen suddenly, as if she'd just woken up.

All she could say was, "Oh!"

And then oh and oh and oh, again and again when Amanda stretched herself out on the pillows, a vision of silk sliding on skin, her breasts pushed together so that they were all cleavage as she held Luce's thighs apart and started those small mouth movements again, lips and tongue on Luce's lips and clit, now kissing parts of Iggy's still-hardening cock, then helping him with the lift and fall of Luce's ass, helping him burrow deeper, tentative at first and then as dominant as any alpha male had ever been, filling her completely, brushing the top of her G-spot, and suddenly they were all moving.

Luce turned around to face Iggy, riding him hard, while Amanda pressed her breasts against Luce's back, she and Iggy kissing hotly over Luce's shoulder until Amanda, shy Amanda, began a low running commentary:

"God that pussy tastes good. I could eat that pussy for breakfast, lunch and dinner. And the way he's fucking you, I can see how deep he's going, oh my Lord, that cock is *huge*, Iggy – look at me," she said, she was so urgent, and then Luce could feel Amanda's own pussy, soft and wet against her ass, and she reached behind to touch it, making Amanda's breath hitch high and fast, and then she was coming, oh God it was happening, it was really happening, she kept saying "I'm coming, fuck me, please, fuck me, fuck me!"

The waves were long and intense, making her shudder over and over again, making her pull off Iggy's swollen cock just in time to see him spurt all over her stomach, hot and salty and sweet when she put her fingers in it and licked them off.

"My turn," Amanda said then, and Iggy leaned back, he motioned her upward.

"Come park that pussy on my face, little girl," he said, adjusting the pillows under his neck, and without a second's hesitation, Amanda knelt over him and slowly lowered herself, reaching for Luce's hands, their fingers intertwined as she manipulated herself against Iggy's open mouth, his tongue a wriggling fish that kept finding the right hidden nooks, making the girl moan which in turn made Luce moan.

She turned herself so that one of Iggy's hands could reach her, and he plunged two, then three fingers in and just like that, she was coming again, in complete tune with Amanda who was hugely vocal, so loud she almost screamed, which made Iggy start to laugh, and then they were all laughing again, laughing and coming and laughing, pressing their faces together, kissing and tasting each other, kissing and finally sighing, the laughter dying down, the waves receding, the juices beginning to dry sticky on their thighs, their faces, their breasts and balls.

They lay there quietly, at ease in the sudden new intimacy, some part of each touching some part of the others.

"I'm so glad I walked into that Golden place!" Amanda said fervently as they lay intertwined, Luce's head on Iggy's stomach, Amanda playing with his dreads, her fingers so dreamy in his hair he had to close his eyes "You are the most beautiful woman I have been with in – well, since I was in love with Sienna," Amanda said then.

Iggy nodded vigorously, Luce could feel his body shaking, and she laughed.

"You were with Sienna, too?"

"Don't joke," he said, his voice quiet, one hand reaching down to grip her hair in a kind of vise.

Liars, Luce thought, so, so fondly. My beautiful liars.

Apparently San Francisco still was that golden place, where magical acts of unsuspected ardor could spark in the space of an evening. She would never, she vowed to herself for the hundred thousandth time, leave this city.

When people talk about "food porn," they mean those over-the-top foodie posts on Instagram, where it's all about exotic ingredients and finicky plating. That's because they haven't read Rose Mark, who connects the primal pleasure of food with another of our deepest pleasure drives. Mark is a true food lover, on and off the page, as well as an inventive and divine cook.

Rose K. Mark

IT'S NOT THAT I'M HUNGRY

Sometimes I like to spread soft butter
Onto the whites of a warm crusty baguette.
Just to see that sweet yellowness
Melt, flow and drool into those pillowy caverns.
It's not that I'm hungry.

Sometimes I like to peel a ripe banana
Undressing it slowly
Sweet and erect
White and inviting
It's not that I'm hungry.

Sometimes I like to crush, smell
Wild greens, sour grass,
Imagining its sour, bitter bite
Between my lips
The fold of my tongue
It's not that I'm hungry.

Sometimes I like to pour my honey eyes
Over a tired old Italian man
Just to see his grey heart lift
In anticipation, memories.

It warms my smile.
It's not that I'm hungry.

It's just for the sight,

Just for the sight.

Stella Fosse is a sixty-something technical writer who came alive sexually in her late fifties. She writes about the joys and absurdities of arriving at the party just when other folks are packing up to go home. She's the founder of Elderotica, a gathering of women in the San Francisco Bay Area dedicated to playful, luscious writing. This story is defiantly honest about the power of sex to change us in every way, and it's shamelessly hot. It will make you want to find your own cowboy or cowgirl pronto.

TERRAFORMING

She was reading Margaret Atwood when Jack walked into the Berkeley café, half an hour late, blinking like an owl. He was new to Bay Area rush hour.

"Lots of traffic," he said.

He was tall and slender and muscular, his white-blonde hair cropped close like a helmet. His face had a fine symmetry. His limbs were long.

They shared one of those awkward coffee date hugs you do before you even know if you can stand the person. Then they sat at her rickety table and traded stories. She was a technical writer, a little woman in big glasses who kept her grey hair black. He was a tradesman, a union man. Every year he pulled his trailer behind a pickup across the country to build a new factory. He was a rock hound in his spare time. A couple of times, he mentioned how big he was, in a cautionary tone that puzzled her. So he was tall; so she was short. No need to belabor the obvious.

"I'll be around all year," he said. "If you ever want to play, I have a real nice place, a trailer in a mobile park in Hayward. And I just got a big TV. It was a return. I got a great deal."

She could tell from his rueful expression that he did not expect to see her again. She was surprised he was interested. He was not her usual type, but she could hardly be his type either: a bluestocking in her sixties, a decade his senior. He kissed her goodnight as they left the café, a dry kiss, the kiss of a guy who hunts rocks. She shivered. He held her gaze.

"You would be fun," he said.

"How do you know?" she asked.

"I just do," he said.

She called a week later and drove south to see him. Her tired heart wanted an intermission. Maybe he was it.

He phoned while she was on her way, told her the best route in a soothing voice. She climbed the steps to his trailer door. He drew her inside, hugged her and sat her down in a comfortable chair. She could see his shoulder blades from across the room, stretching the material of his shirt as he trimmed his nails. He had the knuckles of a workingman. He moved like a big tall cat.

In bed he removed his clothes in one practiced move, like peeling a wrapper off a stick of butter. His beauty astonished her, except "beauty" was too womanly a word. She had been with guys, she had been with nerds, but here was a man. She ran her fingers down his cock, and when she got to where she expected it to end, there was that much all over again.

Now he was on top of her, he kissed her a little, he teased her with his cock. He bit her right nipple, hard, almost hard enough, and then he was inside her cunt and biting her at the same time and she was screaming. She wanted to scream way louder but the man had neighbors.

He worried he would hurt her, because other women didn't like being bitten that hard. *I'm not them! I'm me! Bite hard!* she was thinking, and then he bit her left breast. Not her nipple, but the side of her breast, hard, and that actually did hurt. Her boobs weren't made of steel after all.

He rolled onto his back and put her on top, sitting astride him, and she stopped thinking. Which was what she craved, the blessing of temporary monkey-mind shutdown, just brain stem, just pussy grinding on dick. This part she only remembered vaguely, later, the feeling of taking him over and over, her vulva gripping him like the mouth of a fish closing and opening, and his blue eyes, wide, while he said, "I like feeling you come."

A week later she knocked on the door again, and Jack said, "Come in."

His voice wasn't that deep, wasn't the bass you might expect from such a man, but it was deeply resonant. It certainly resonated in her.

She walked in and he was almost naked, only in jockey shorts. "I'm just getting out of the shower," he said, "just the way you like me."

"I'd like you any way," she said, "hairy or smooth, clean or dirty."

She was wearing a jump suit and he didn't like how hard it was to take it off. He lay on top of her in bed, he entered her and looked into her eyes and said, "That's a well-behaved pussy. Your pussy is being good tonight." And as he moved in her, he said, "I want you to relax. Open up your pussy all the way."

"What?"

"Just think about it being open. That's it," and then, after a minute, "Okay, now squeeze me."

And as open as she was, the only squeezing she could do was deep inside, and when she tried, she came, way deep in her vagina. And she kept coming as he kept moving. He had this look on his face, so satisfied, and he said again, "I like feeling you come."

They fucked and fucked. Sometimes he got soft enough to fit down her throat. Sometimes she yelled, sometimes she was quiet. Sometimes she was on top, sometimes she was complete jelly and had to lie down. After he came, they lay in bed, and he told her about his boss at the construction site getting mad because he took off one glove to use the phone.

"You're supposed to have both gloves on at all times," said the boss.

"Yeah well unlike you I don't hold my dick in my gloves when I piss," said Jack.

What a different thing it must be, to be a man among men when your cock is twice the size of anybody else's.

In the dark she rubbed the top of his head, his grey-blonde hair thick and short. "I live up here, almost all the time," she said. "That's why I like sex. It brings me down here," and she rubbed the back of his skull, just above his hairline.

"I always live down there," he said.

"Must be nice," she said.

He told her to watch two porn films in the coming week, beginning to end. That was her homework. It amused her to think of having sex homework in her sixties. Then they got up, showered and dressed, and sat in his living room. He put on some comedy show for a few minutes, and then turned it off.

"I have one more assignment for you before you go," he said, walking back into his bedroom.

"Should I come in there?" she asked.

"Yes," he said. She walked in as he took off his shirt. Then he handed her his skin ointment and asked her to put some on the part of his back where he couldn't reach. She laughed.

"I thought this was going to be sexy," she said. "You're teasing me." But of course touching his back was sexy.

"The only reason nothing is happening is because you're wearing a unitard," he said, and peeled it off her. He bent her over the bed and fucked her from the back until her legs collapsed, and then she lay on her belly on the bed and he kept going. He wore out, and she lay on top of him, relaxing her pussy and then holding on and coming like he had taught her.

"Is this too much?" She asked him.

"Oh baby, just keep going," he said, and at last he came again and asked for some air. She rolled off and they were quiet for a bit. She got up and dressed, kissed his dick, and left him wiped out and naked on his bed.

It was midnight. It had been five hours. What an absolute gift.

In bed one night, he tied her hands to his headboard and teased her for a long time. Fingers on her G spot, then spanked her. She wrapped her legs around his and pulled him toward her, but he wasn't budging. Finally he slid into her, just a little bit, moving, on top, holding his upper body away with his arms, looking into her eyes, a serious look on his face. Then he came all the way in.

"Bring her out," he said.

"What do you mean?" she said.

"Bring out your clit and kiss my cock."

"I don't know what you're talking about," she said.

"Kiss my cock with your clit," he said.

And her body did it even though her brain didn't know what he meant. She felt her clit extend all the way, push against his big cock as he slid in and out. She was exposed in a way she had never been, and her cunt started kissing him too, squeezing and squeezing over and over. They looked each other in the eye as it went on, she coming and coming, and it was almost painful, the sensation of friction on her clit.

"I'm going slow, so she knows I won't hurt her," he said. But after a while, he sped up and *she* (this part of her that was now a separate *she*, with a will of her own) retracted a little bit. Still wonderful but not that thing, that amazing thing she had just learned she could do at the age of sixty-one.

"I've never felt you come like that," he said later. "That was incredible."

When she left he said, "Thanks for doing what I asked."

She laughed. "Thanks for asking me."

"Funny that you and I have never talked politics," she said one night, right after they walked into his bedroom.

She regretted her words the instant they left her mouth. Here they had this nice arrangement, just sex – like dessert with no vegetables. What did she expect would happen? A guy from Montana and a Berkeley gal. Next thing she knew, he was talking guns.

"Anybody who wants to take my guns away deserves to get shot with them," he said. She tried not to take this personally, figuring he didn't exactly mean her, yet imagining a bullet in her back if she tried to flee his trailer. Anyway, what was he really talking about when he talked about guns? If it was his dick, she didn't want to take it away, just borrow it sometimes.

They sat on his bed, and he opened a closet door. He reached for an upper shelf and took down a camouflage bag. Behind it were two pistols. They were in holders. He put them on the bed, reverently. She thought maybe he wanted her to pick them up but she didn't touch them.

"Do they have bullets?" She asked.

"Yes," he said.

"Better keep them away from kids," she said.

"How many kids do you see in this trailer?" he asked, exasperated.

Then he said guns were "fun." The word he always used about sex. He showed her a video of his son shooting a repeating rifle into a pumpkin full of explosives and blowing it up, pieces everywhere, car alarms blaring a block away. He loved it.

Then he put his guns back in the closet. They lay down, side by side, staring at the ceiling. He was naked. She had everything on but her shoes. She could not stop thinking that those guns had been there, in that closet, every time she came to see him.

"I want some boobs," he said.

"I can't figure out whether to take off my clothes or get up and go," she said.

"I'm gonna shoot you with some blanks," he said, reaching for her. *Oh brother,* she thought. *A vasectomy gun joke.*

She lay on top of him and said, "We used most of our fuck time talking politics."

"I'm gonna kick you out of here in an hour," he said.

It was harder for her to let him in that night. Once she rolled off and lay on the other side of the bed and he came and found her, his cock coming into her pussy from behind.

"No matter where I go, there you are," she said.

In reality, she thought, *there is no such thing as casual sex.*

In the dark afterward, he talked about women he had known who could not tolerate his size. One in particular, who had fainted when he entered her.

"I am not a monster," he said into the night.

At home in her own bed, she dreamt she was out in space.

Naked, legs wide apart, hair floating, blotting out the stars.

Comets, planets, even suns seemed like tiny little lights.

She swallowed them all with her pussy as she passed.

Next time she was with him, late in the dark, she told him about her dream. He thought for a minute.

"Well," he said, "I like it better than that other dream you had."

"What other dream?" she asked.

"The one where we had a picnic on my kitchen floor and you left without fucking me," he said.

"Oh yeah," she said, "*that* dream."

Another time, after they had fucked a few minutes, he put her on top, astride him.

"Is this the part where I ask for what I want?" She said, looking down at him.

"Sure."

"I want you to fuck me from behind and touch my clit."

"OK. Can I tell you what I want?"

"Yes," she said.

"Next time you come over," he said, "I want you to shave your pussy first."

She had always kept her hair, but he was shaved, and he had brought this up before. She was willing to try. "We don't have to wait," she said. "I could do that now."

"No," he said, "I want to do it." He rolled her onto the mattress and got up. Without her glasses she could just make out his silhouette in the dim light as he gathered razor and scissors and shaving cream, and ran water into a little bowl.

"You've done this for someone before," she guessed.

He paused a second. "Yes."

He lay down next to her legs, opened them and began to shave, carefully, deliberately.

"You're going to love this," he said. "Everything will feel different. Underwear will feel different."

When he cut the hair on her labia with scissors, she got nervous. "This requires a certain level of trust," she said.

"Yes," he said.

"It's kind of like being at the beauty parlor, only not quite. I had a facial last weekend," she said. "The woman who did it does Brazilians too. She told me that in Brazil, girls start getting Brazilians when they have their first period."

"I believe it," he said, still shaving.

She rattled on nervously while he worked, deliberately, slowly.

When he finished, he handed her a mirror, just like a hairdresser would. Only what she saw wasn't *short* hair. What she saw was – *no* hair. Her sixty-one-year-old labia, naked for the first time since puberty. She laughed, amazed. "I have to get up and rinse the soap off."

"Don't move, I've got you," he said, and wiped her down gently, with a cloth dipped in warm water. He put the shaving things aside, lay on top of her, and looked her in the eye.

"Now I'm going to fuck a shaved pussy," he said.

It was instantly different. There was nothing to hold him back, not even a little. He moved the tiniest bit and slid inside. And when he went all the way in, it was not just cock fucking vagina, it was the skin around his cock fucking the skin around her vagina. There was suction: skin itself holding on and letting go. She couldn't get enough. She rode him, and rode some more.

The next day she walked down a busy sidewalk. Tiny hairs starting to grow back on her labia caught the weave of her underwear and pulled her pussy back and forth as she walked. As if she were fucking the street and everybody on it. She loved it.

The next time she saw him, she thanked him.

"There's suction when you fuck me," she said. "It pulls on my clit every time you move."

"It isn't just about slippery," he said. "Sometimes it's sticky and you stick together. Sometimes it's dry and rough."

He knew a lot, this one. He was a connoisseur of fuck.

Because he was so big, when she first knew him she got headaches and uterine cramps the morning after she fucked him. But no longer: Things had shifted inside her to make room. She'd been terraformed. And more than that: After watching him at the wheel of his pickup, she got wet whenever some guy in a truck passed her on the freeway. She'd been conditioned, like one of Pavlov's flipping dogs.

One night they lay on their sides, he behind her. He tried to go into her butt. It hurt, maybe the position. They turned over so she was on her belly and he came into her, gradually. "Ow," she said, and he slowed down but did not stop. He knew she could do this, had more faith than she did. There was that moment when she could not understand how it could actually happen, and then he was in, he was sliding into her so big all the way up. Oh God. She was way past worrying what the neighbors thought, she was yowling like a cat.

"You like this," he said, and then he was moving hard and fast, in a way she never thought possible in her ass, his big cock in and out. It was incredible, over and over. And then she hit some limit, and the sound she made changed from a woman in passion to something more like a kid with a scraped knee.

"You done?" he said.

"Mm-hmm" she said in a high voice. He turned her on her side but did not come out.

"Just relax," he said, "take a rest. Good. Now. Move a little bit. I'm just going to lie here. *You* move."

She did move a little and it was so good and almost too much. No, it was too much, how could she do this? But how could she not move, when it felt the way it felt? She stopped and started, moaning and saying no, moaning more, reaching for him.

He stayed still. "This is all *you* doing this, you know," he said.

"No it's not. You're so big, oh–" She was not exactly articulate. When she pushed against him, she impaled her ass on him, again and again, while he lay there waiting.

"Funny how you can want it and not want it," he said.

"Yes!" she said, then lapsed into moans.

Finally she was really done, finally her butt could not take another moment.

"You did incredibly well," he said, as if she had climbed a mountain. He stood, took off the rubber, cleaned himself, then wiped her ass with a damp cloth.

"Thank you, very kind," she mumbled.

He chuckled. "Least I can do, after what I did to you," he said. Only he didn't do it, she did it.

She turned over onto her back. "I'm in a coma," she said.

"That's fine. You just lie there and be in a coma." He climbed on top. She could not move. She was so wet it was running onto his bedspread. He slid into her pussy. Above her, his face got that look, that distant absorbed look, and he fucked and fucked, grunting sometimes. She wanted to be quiet so he could concentrate, but soon she couldn't help but make noise and move up to meet him. So much for the coma.

He sweated. Drops hit her face. "Sorry," he said, got up to grab a towel, came back inside. At the end he got even bigger, even thicker, pushing out the edges of her pussy until he groaned and she felt the shift in his balls, movement of semen through tubes and out.

Then he was on the other side of the bed, apologizing again, this time for being way over there. Heat came off him in waves.

"It's amazing how good that makes you feel," he said.

She showered, he showered. She put on clothes, he put on pajamas. She wanted to thank him for mending her old broken heart. For teaching her how to make boundaries and protect her feelings, even in passion. For the great lesson that it's not just possible, but a very good thing, to be friends with someone who is not like you. But she didn't know how to say that stuff without sounding sentimental, so she just kissed his cheek and headed for the door.

"See you soon," he said, and she said goodnight.

She woke the next morning expecting to be sore, but was not. Not at all. She had a deep sense of having been with a man. At work her friend LJ told her some stupid thing that was happening in her department, then walked up close and said in her Chicago accent, "You look beautiful today. Different. I wonder what it is." Pretty LJ, also in her sixties, who went home every night to an empty house.

She thought – but didn't say – *It's terraforming.*

Jan Steckel's poetry is mind-blowingly inventive, so it
wasn't such a big surprise when I cyberstalked her and
found that she'd graduated from Radcliffe (at the time,
Harvard's sister school), studied Golden Age Spanish
Literature at Oxford University and then got her MD from
Yale School of Medicine. Don't ask how she went on to win
a 2012 Lambda Literary Award for Bisexual Nonfiction.
Just be glad you get to read this poem.

Jan Steckel

SEDER WITH MY OCTAROON

Since God declared that on this night
the Jews should eat while they recline,
let me happily lie supine
and lick your asshole with delight.

Though you're seven-eighths a goy,
the eighth part must religious be,
observant of God's least decree,
so sit on my face, my darling boy.

Every time you squeeze my hand,
moan in ecstatic reverie,
you inch away from Calvary
closer to the Promised Land.

Beth Elliott is a journalist, author and activist who helped create the West Coast Lesbian Conference in 1973 and co-founded San Francisco's Alice B. Toklas LGBT Club. For these and many other achievements, she was recognized as one of the "Feminists Who Changed America, 1963–1975" (University of Illinois Press, 2015). On the creative front, she's been a folk musician since the 1960s, has written for magazines and newspapers and authored four books, including the science-fiction novel *Don't Call It "Virtual"* and her recently completed experimental erotic fiction collection, *The Smart Drug Masochists*.

On Facebook, she's posted the motto, "When in trouble, when in doubt, run in circles, scream and shout." But her protagonists are braver than that – as we see in the following story, a tale of two friends who aren't afraid to, um, seize the moment.

THE PEACE OFFERING

"Reba, will you get on in here and close that door? You're going to work that air conditioner to death and send the electric bill through the roof."

Reba pulled herself up straight and away from the door frame, brushed a damp wisp of frosted hair back from her forehead and replied, "Damn, Charleen, I thought you said my feet would get used to waitressing. It's been four months, and they're just killing me today!"

Charleen, a can of beer in each hand, bumped the refrigerator shut with her behind and said, "A busy day's a busy day." She hande./d Reba one beer, popped the other and took a swig. "And I thought you said you'd done this before, down home in La Grange."

Reba, taking a long pull from her can, took a moment to answer. "That was just a summer job at the Bon Ton, and most folks had the buffet." She lay in the easy chair as limply as she could without spilling her beer and groaned. "If I hadn't have married Freddie, I'd have finished beauty school and wouldn't have to do this."

"Woulda, coulda, shoulda," Charleen replied. "Hold on a minute, I won't be able to hear you." She placed a plastic dishpan in the kitchen sink and started the tap running, then emptied a tray of ice cubes into the pan.

"Here," she said, carrying the now-full pan over to her friend, "lift those feet." She placed the pan down, stood upright and stretched backwards, placing one hand behind her just below the elastic waistband of her skirt. "OK, soak 'em, honey." She listened to Reba's sigh of relief as she picked up her beer again, then continued, "Besides, if you were a hairdresser, you'd still be on your feet all day, and there's no money in doing manicures."

She sat on the arm of the chair and reached over Reba's head to place a comforting hand on her far shoulder. "Anyway," she said, "you know work's harder and feet get sorer when you're nursing a broken heart." Holding onto her beer with a thumb and two fingers, she stroked Reba's other shoulder, leaned over her and softly said, "You know this is the worst part, and you're holding up real good. You've got a whole new life ahead of you, and you are going to be real, real happy."

Reba sighed, "I'm glad you keep reminding me, Charleen. It is real hard. I know I wouldn't have made it without you taking me in an getting' me this job. It's so good of you to do all that just for me."

Charleen leaned over, looked into her friend's face and smiled. "Well, what are friends for?" she asked, and waited for the corners of Reba's mouth to turn upward. "That's better!" She sat back up and said, "Now, let me go out and get the mail so I can kick my shoes off, too. Of course, you may want to leave the room after that, but then I'd get that pan of ice water for my own feet!"

Reba was still laughing when Charleen closed the door behind herself.

When she returned, Charleen carried two envelopes and what looked like a shoe box wrapped in brown paper. "Nothing much in the way of mail," she said, "but that means nothing in the way of a bill, praise Jesus! But the neighbor lady was holding a package for you. Do you want to open it now or after I fix us some supper?"

"My feet and I are staying put. Um, unless you want me to help cook or set the table or something."

"You just sit tight. We've got that tuna salad we've got to finish, remember? I'll just make us a couple of sandwiches, anything but turn on a stove burner in this heat."

"Amen to that! I'm more tired than I am hungry."

Tuna sandwiches, chips and sweet tea proved to be as restorative a meal as it was simple, so Reba got up when they were done and did the dishes. Charleen took a pair of scissors out of a drawer and set them on the table, then brought Reba's package over and sat down.

"So, this doesn't look like mail order, Reba."

Reba came over and sat down opposite Charleen and said, "I'm not expecting anything."

Charleen turned the box till she could see the addresses. "Well, I'll be," she said. "It looks like it's from Freddie."

"Oh, Lord," said Reba, throwing her head back against the chair, "what could he possibly be sending me?" She looked up again, then nearly jumped out of the chair as she screamed, "DON'T SHAKE THAT, CHARLEEN! It could be a bomb for all we know!"

Charleen looked amused as she shook the box near her ear. "Hey, you're the one always saying he's cute, but if brains were gunpowder he couldn't blow his nose. So how's he going to have the brains to put some gunpowder together to blow us up? Besides, Freddie's the hurt puppy-dog kind, not the bitter, nasty kind." She held the box in front of her waist and stared at it. "I can't tell what all's in here. Want me to open it for you?"

"Yes, please," Reba drawled. "I couldn't stand the wait if I had to get up and do it myself, I'm just dying of so much curiosity."

Charleen cut the brown paper and unwrapped the parcel as Reba watched intently. When she lifted the lid of the box inside, she jerked back out of her chair and her eyes went wide. She caught her balance, gasped, and brought a hand over her mouth. Then she slowly leaned forward again, began to giggle as she looked in the box, and finally held her tummy and laughed aloud. "Lord almighty," she cried. "Reba ..." She laughed again. "Reba, you are not going to believe this! This is ... this is so ... so ...”

"What, Charleen, what?"

Charleen had both hands on the table to support herself while she laughed. "Well ... there are two things in here. One looks like it's supposed to be a leather G-string, only it's got a hole in front with a metal ring around it? And the other—well, here, catch!"

Reba raised her head to follow the trajectory of what looked at first like a big rawhide dog chew. But it was softer when she caught it, and floppier, and as she got a closer look she screamed and dropped it. Then she laughed, picked the fake penis off the floor and inspected it, and laughed some more. "What the hell is this supposed to mean?" she exclaimed.

"There's a note here," said Charleen. "I'll read it to you."

"Dear Reba,

"If you are really going to leave me and stay with your girlfriend who if she was your friend would tell you to come back to me, you are going to need this. I hope it will remind you of me and the good times we have had so maybe you

will come back home where you belong.

> *"'Your loving husband,*
> *"'Freddie.'"*

Reba looked at her husband's gift and shook her head. "That man is crazy, and that's a fact."

Charleen laughed even harder. When she could catch her breath, she asked, "So this is what he thinks you'll remember him by. Tell me, Reba, is it a true likeness?"

Reba's sad face brightened. "Oh, maybe in his dreams, Charleen." She started to giggle. "Or maybe, or maybe I could take this into court with me and show it to the judge. I'll say, 'Your honor, Freddie and I agree on what he is and how he treated me.' And the judge will take one look and say, 'Divorce granted!'"

"Ha! Let me see that thing again."

"OK. Now you catch! Ooh, nice catch!"

"Honey, I've been grabbing these things since I was 14. Let me see. Hmmm," Charleen mused after further inspection. "This sure is some funny kind of rubber, or something. Look at it wiggle."

"Just as funny as the real thing," said Reba. "I've never seen nothing like that, and I used to have one of those battery massager things, like they advertise with the girl holding it up to her face?"

"Yeah, this must be real high-class down 'n' dirty stuff. I can't imagine him finding this here in Bakersfield. He must've gone to L.A. for this."

Reba nodded. "Or at least to Fresno."

"Must have. Say," Charleen continued suspiciously, "if he misses you so much, what's he doing driving down to L.A. looking to get his peter pulled?"

"Like he always says, Charleen, when a man works hard he's got to have his fun. And that he wants his woman to have nothing but the best. Of course, the having fun part comes first, even if it means there's nothing left over for the 'woman having the best' part." Reba took the toy from Charleen and shook her head. "And when he finally does both ..."

"Well," Charleen yawned, "he sure made our evening. Just not in the way he expected. But I'm ready to drop. Let's skip the television and get us some sleep."

"Sounds good to me!"

When Reba's fitful rolling woke her up, Charleen heard her either sighing or moaning repeatedly. "Reba, what's the matter?" she asked. "You aren't having another nightmare, are you?"

"No," Reba whined, her voice quivering. "I just couldn't sleep. I feel so scared about my life. And I found myself missing how Freddie used to comfort me when I woke up in the middle of the night. He'd hold me and start making love to me, and I'd forget about whatever was bothering me."

"Oh, no, Reba!" Charleen switched on a lamp by the bed, then put one arm under Reba's neck and pulled her close. "You can't let yourself miss him, honey. You know in the morning your troubles'd still be there, and he's trouble number one. Here, I'll hold you till you feel better." She gently brought Reba's head to her chest and stroked her hair as Reba hugged her tightly. "If he gets the notion you can't give him up, he'll never leave you be. You could be trapped for the rest of your life, girl."

"It's not Freddie I miss," said Reba, shaking her head as much as she could with it resting on Charleen's bosom. "I figured it out, right before you woke up. What it is, is it's such a comfort to feel all filled up inside while wrapping my arms and legs around somebody and holding on? That's what I'm missing."

Charleen put her head back and looked up at the ceiling, saying nothing, so Reba continued, "I don't want to want Freddie for that. And I don't want to bring home some oil-well jockey or honky-tonk cowboy to go to town on me and fall asleep just when he's done, leaving me lying there feeling just as lonesome as before." She looked up at Charleen and found her still staring upward, as though she wanted to look a little further off than the ceiling would allow. "What're you thinking, Charleen?"

"Oh, well ..." She sighed. "I was thinking how right you are about the comforting. And about the honky-tonks. Lord, do I know how right you are!"

Reba waited a moment, then asked, "And what else?"

"Hunh?"

"What else were you thinking about?" She waited again, then, impatiently, said, "Come on, Charleen, tell me! I know you're thinking about something."

"Well ... I was just thinking ..." Charleen sighed and turned her face toward her friend. "You know, I'd feel downright silly, but ... oh, never mind."

"Char-LEE-een!" Reba propped herself on one elbow and protested, "TELL me!"

Charleen turned on her side to face her, but lowered her gaze. "I just had this stupid thought about how much better I could make you feel with ... well, there was that little present from Freddie, and ... oh, you probably think that's strictly from dumb!"

Reba suddenly lay very still; when she spoke, it was almost with reverence. "Charleen? You mean you'd do that for me? Just to make me feel better?"

Charleen looked up at her sheepishly. "Well, you are my best friend. And you know it tears me up inside to see you hurting. Enough to come up with a dumb idea like that!"

"I don't think it's dumb at all. I think it's real sweet of you."

"You do?"

"I do. And you don't have to worry about feeling silly, 'cause we know it's 'cause you're my friend just trying to comfort me, not any funny stuff."

Charleen's eyebrows rose. "You mean you really want me to get that thing and ..."

"Well, I kinda ... I kinda want ... It'd be a real comfort to me, Charleen. Specially getting to feel that ... knowing I'm safe, I'm with a girlfriend, and not taking my chances with some strange man." Slowly, her whole body relaxed and, with a calm look spreading over her face as she realized what she'd just said, she simply asked, "Please?"

"Well, of course, if you really want me to," Charleen replied without hesitation. "You always could talk me into doing the silliest things."

Nonetheless, as she pulled back the covers, sat up, and felt around with her feet for her slippers, she let out a quiet "Lord, have mercy!" She stood up and said, "I think we left the box on the kitchen table." Then she walked to the door, where she turned to say, "But you've got to get yourself ready, Reba. I love you, but I ain't about to romance you."

"Oh, that's no problem," Reba replied with a grin. "I was hot to trot before I woke you up."

Reba sat up in bed, hiked up the night shirt with the iron-on "Harley Davidson—Made in America" design on the front, and began to run a hand back and forth over breasts the size and shape of navel oranges. Her other hand began wandering up one thigh and down the other, sometimes lightly brushing the moist flesh barely peeking out from the tuft of curly hair between the two. With each "Dang!" or "Doggone it!" from elsewhere in the trailer, she let go of her breasts in favor of grabbing a shoulder and scrunching up in a hug she mentally sent to her friend.

Finally, a voice from just outside the bedroom asked, "OK, are you ready for this? 'Cause I'm not so sure I am!"

"Yeah, I'm ready," Reba drawled. "Let's get a look at the stud-muffinette here."

Charleen tiptoed in, eight inches of faux penis peeking out from under the hem of her baby doll top. "Don't you make fun of me now," she said. "You know I'm a virgin when it comes to this."

"Hey, girl," said Reba, "there ain't nothing like a good-looking hunk, but I think I like that big ol' hard-on better without the attitude attached?"

Charleen stood a little taller and her eyes widened. "You mean this is actually okay?"

Reba looked her up and down, cocked her head and grinned. "Yeah ... it is. It's real different. But ... friendly."

Charleen, losing her bashfulness to the point of working on a proud little smirk, started to strut slowly over to the bed, noting the bounce of her proxy dong as she did. "Well, maybe you should try this on some time, like under that little black velvet skirt of yours? Then invite Freddie over. He'll think you couldn't live without his, then you can show him yours!"

Reba laughed. "That'd be a real hoot! But forget ol' Freddie. Do something for me, Charleen? Hitch up that baby doll for me a minute?"

Charleen went ahead and took it off. "How's this?"

"Unh-huh! Damn, but you're a sight! Those cute little titties and that big ol' hoofloppy! It's downright precious." Reba blushed. "And kind of a turn-on, too!"

"Well, said Charleen optimistically, "I guess I don't have to worry too much about this working, then." She made her way on her knees across the bed to position herself between Reba's legs. "Here, let me scoot on up here," she said. "Oops, better let me move back just a tad." She propped herself up with stiffened arms. "I think this'll do. Can you help me in?"

"Well, can you try aiming it with one hand?"

"I guess. OK," Charleen whispered. "I think this is it." Feeling its head securely inside, she balanced herself on her hands again and let her hips slide the dildo in. Then she gently lowered herself down on top of her friend, laying a forearm on either side of Reba's rib cage.

"Oh, sweet Jesus, that feels good, Charleen!" Reba threw her head back and let her legs fall to the bed, but drew her knees up enough that her feet rested flat on the mattress. "Ohhh ..." she moaned, as Charleen tried out a slow rhythm and became less tentative with her thrusting. "Oh, yes, that's it!"

"Good. Ungh!"

"Is something wrong, Charleen?"

"Not really wrong ... You know, when I push in, the place down there this thing presses against? It's ... just the right spot." She laughed. "It just happens to feel real good when I give it to you."

"Well, all right, girl! No wonder you're doing real good. I didn't know it could work for you, too, but I'm glad it does."

"Yeah," exclaimed Charleen breathily. "You better watch it, though—I just may get inspired here."

Reba giggled. "Oh, I hope so!" And she let out a gasp as Charleen leaned on her elbows to adjust her position, getting deeper inside in the process.

Minding Reba's breathing and the rhythm of her body, Charleen started varying her motion just a little, adding some side-to-side movement, getting Reba to where the little moans started escaping her mouth even as her own breathing began to deepen.

After a while, Reba, who was stroking Charleen's hair and peppering her cheeks with little kisses, caught enough of her breath to cry, "Dang, Charleen, this is so good! And you just keep on a'going, too! Freddie would have been done by now."

"Just paying attention," Charleen gasped. That's all. Except ... well ... I didn't know it'd be such a thrill, getting you all worked up like this."

"Yeah," Reba panted, "you are breathing pretty heavy yourself."

"When I push and that thing keeps hitting me down there, it feels like touching myself. It feels really good when I push it inside you. It feels so good, I keep forgetting ... "

"OHHHHH!" The wave of Reba's orgasm was sweeping her away, and Charleen held on for the ride, thrusting harder and faster to ride that wave and keep it coming. "Oh, Charleen! Yes!"

Happy as she was at her friend's pleasure, Charleen felt all the love she had for Reba wash over her heart at once, which brought tears to form at the corner of her eyes. But when the wave subsided and her friend's body calmed down, Charleen was still moving inside her frantically and gasping for air. "Good Lord, Reba," she panted, as Reba relaxed her arms from around her neck (not without another flurry of kisses on her cheeks and lips). "I could've just died the way your body was pushing this thing against me." She caught her breath, but was still moving inside her friend at more than idling speed. "You know, honey," she whispered, "I feel so close to you right now."

Reba nodded vigorously, and pulled her knees up further and spread her legs wider, drawing Charleen's body in till it was right against hers. As she locked her legs around Charleen, their breasts met nipple to nipple, sending a sensation through both of them, making them both gasp.

Face to face now, they kissed on the lips—a kiss which drew them in to parting their lips and letting their tongues speak for them inside each other's mouth.

Charleen's thrusting became more intent and expressive now. She spread her knees further apart on the bed; this took her deeper inside the pulsating chamber which opened wider to take her in. It also opened her wider as though for penetration, even as she took her friend deeper into ecstasy, moving the dildo in and out like an extension of her own body. Another wave came over Reba, and another, and yet another.

"Oh, Charleen!" Reba cried. "Oh, honey! I never knew it didn't stop after it ... after the first one was over!"

Charleen gasped like a runner for breath. "Reba ... I think I can feel this thing inside you ... and I think it's gonna go off on me. I feel ... I feel something really intense down there, building up ... "

"Are you OK? Do you need to stop?"

"I can't stop! Oh! Ohhhh!" A string of high-pitched whimpers filled the room as Charleen thrust into Reba again and again, completely at the mercy of the violent spasming of her clitoris.

It felt so good: she felt it deep inside herself, she felt she was feeling it inside her friend, it was so crazy and so good her mind went away and she started crying. As her orgasm subsided and she collapsed on top of Reba, her cries became soft whimpers.

Reba held her friend till her body relaxed. She rolled the two of them over, the dildo falling out of her as she did so, and lay down on the bed. Charleen kept whimpering softly, as though she were able to let go of being strong for the both of them and make peace with exhaustion.

Reba nestled her friend's head on her own breasts. When the sounds Charleen was making faded into contented sighs, Reba put a pillow under Charleen's head and gently began undoing the belt.

"Reba?"

"Yes, honey?"

"That was beautiful," Charleen whispered.

"Oh, yes, indeed," Reba replied as she reached for some tissues and patted Charleen's soaking wet vulva with them. "That was very beautiful. And you know what? I think you needed the comforting of it as much as I did. Or at least, you got it, too."

Charleen reached up and stroked Reba's arm. "I reckon so."

Reba finished tending to Charleen, wiped herself dry, and pulled the covers over the two of them.

"Reba?" said Charleen as Reba reached for the light. "You know, we really ought to write Freddie a nice thank-you note for that wonderful present."

Reba chuckled softly. "After the divorce is final, honey," she said, and turned out the light.

Dorothy Freed's writing is informed by a long and happy sex life. Leaving an early, unsatisfying marriage, she arrived in San Francisco in time to be an enthusiastic participant in the sexual revolution. She told an interviewer, "I had fucked enough men for a small, sex-starved country."

Her erotica has appeared in numerous anthologies; on her blog, *Sixty-Nine and Still Sexual*, she writes about her thirty-two-years-long relationship with Sir, her husband and BDSM top, and what it's like to be now 71 and still sexual.

Her contribution to this anthology has a very happy ending – the kind we all wish for.

FULL BODY MASSAGE

After shattering my left ankle last Memorial Day, I was forced to spend the summer in a knee-high plaster cast. To say that this cramped my style was an understatement, since, at age fifty-two, I was twice-divorced, hot to trot, and unfortunately between lovers. By mid-July, I was completely cranky from inactivity, with my entire body sore and out of alignment from dragging myself around on crutches. And in spite of being blessed with a pretty face, dark wavy hair, and a still-shapely figure, I hadn't been laid in months. In fact, the only man to approach me with the cast on my leg had a kinky hospital fantasy that did not turn me on.

My best friend Joel, who's gay, took pity on me and showed up one evening at my flat, with an impish grin on his smooth-shaven, cherubic face. "I have a *surprise* for you Mia," he trilled, "and it's *just* what you *need*."

Then, smiling mysteriously, he helped me downstairs to his car and drove us to a lavender Victorian in the Castro, home and workplace of his friend Don, a lesbian—and according to Joel—"the *absolutely* best masseuse in San Francisco."

Don (short for Donna) was a tall butch in her late

fifties, small breasted and narrow-hipped, with strong, muscular arms. She met us at the door wearing a wife-beater undershirt and black exercise pants. Her short silvery hair was brushed back from her angular, high-cheek-boned face and she wore no makeup. My green eyes met her brown ones. We held our gaze for a moment, then she flashed me a friendly smile, and I decided I liked her.

In spite of the cast on my leg, I felt relaxed just sitting and sipping tea in Don's peaceful living room with its oak furnishings and Asian area rugs. There was soft lighting, meditation music, and the pleasing scent of sandalwood in the air. Across the room to the right of the front window were a black padded massage table and a bottle of fragrant oil.

Joel's surprise turned out to be the gift of a two-hour massage.

He soon set down his teacup and excused himself, "Well, I'm off to the Café Flora for coffee and flirtation. I'm leaving you in the *best* of hands, sweetie," he promised, grinning. "I'll pick you up later. Enjoy."

"Are there any tender or painful body parts I should be aware of?" Don inquired before beginning the massage.

I lay naked, face down on her padded massage table, covered by a light blanket. I sighed. "That's pretty much *any* body part you can name after six weeks in this cast."

"Why you poor woman," she said, in a low, husky voice, "You *are* in need of attention, aren't you? Let's see if I can make you feel better."

Don poured a small circle of heated massage oil into her hands and rubbed her palms together, releasing a soothing, spicy smell into the air. She began with basic Swedish massage, combined with acupressure; first working on my tension-filled upper arms and shoulders, then moving down my spine to my achy lower back, and then to my hips.

I felt the first small twinges of arousal between my legs when Don's hands, slick with oil, slid over the smooth round cheeks of my ass, stroking, kneading and spreading them apart. The sensations became so exciting that I squirmed with pleasure, surprising myself, because I wasn't into women at all. But Don was tall, broad-shouldered, and somehow manly, particularly in the dim light of the room—and into women or not, this massage was turning me on.

I grew increasingly aroused as Don continued to massage my hips and ass. I began to imagine, what if those talented hands were to slide between my legs, parting the swollen outer lips of my opening... and delve into the moist tingling flesh within? I waited, barely breathing, but then she moved on to the backs of my thighs and knees and then downward to my lower legs, and spent some time doing acupressure on my feet.

Calm down, Mia, I told myself, *what are you*

expecting anyway—a full body massage?

"Mia, you can turn over now," Don said softly.

Struggling with the cast, I rolled myself over and, with the blanket covering me, I lay back comfortably with a small pillow beneath my neck. Using her fingertips, Don massaged my head, face, and throat, even my ears, and the muscles in my arms and hands.

"You're really tense. You need to remember to breathe," she said firmly, continuing on to stroke my neck, and shoulders and upper chest.

I was breathing alright, half gasping in fact, with my nipples jutting out at attention, breasts aching with excitement, and the muscles of my pussy clenching and squeezing down hard. Never mind becoming less sexual during menopause—by the time Don reached my lower belly, I was ready, more than ready for anything she wanted to do.

But she folded the blanket back over me, and her hands moved onto my thighs instead, and continued downward to my knees, lower legs, and feet—and then slowly, deliberately, back up again.

She paused when her hands reached the tops of my thighs, with her fingertips almost but not quite brushing my pubic curls hidden beneath the blanket. A hot rush of excitement traveled like an electric current straight to my clit. I gasped with pleasure and opened my eyes.

Don gazed down at me longingly. "Beautiful Mia,"

she murmured and waited, her dark eyes questioning. Speechless with excitement, I smiled up at her and nodded my agreement. *Full body massage, oh my god, yes! Please don't stop now!* I thought, and a ripple of pleasure went through my entire body when she set the blanket aside and reached for me.

Smiling her delight, she cupped my full breasts in her hands and then reached for my swollen nipples, clamping and twisting them between thumbs and forefingers, making me moan. Then her warm, strong hands slid down over my hips and the slope of my belly, raising my excitement level still higher.

When she finally went down on me, I wanted it so much I was panting like a dog and spreading my legs wide in anticipation. Don's tongue was warm and wet and knowing as she delved into my folds. There was no blundering here and zero confusion about the location of my clit—she knew exactly where it was and how to pleasure it. Slowly, expertly, she licked and sucked and teased and nibbled for what seemed like a long time, until I was moaning with pleasure, head tossing, hips bucking, back arching and inner muscles squeezing down.

Finally she slid her hands beneath me, separating my ass cheeks and massaging the responsive flesh around my tight little rear opening. That touch was unexpected and made me so hot I knew I was close to coming. Reaching out, I caressed her hair.

"Please, please don't stop." I whispered urgently—

and bless her, she didn't.

I moaned in delight as tension mounted until every nerve in my body felt alive with sensation, and the exquisite feelings intensified and enveloped me. When I finally exploded, toes curling and screaming with release, it was one of those monumental orgasms that went on and on and on.

When I opened my eyes, I realized that Don had covered me with the blanket again and left the room. Dazed, I got up and slowly dressed myself, hardly believing what had just happened. I couldn't stop smiling.

Don reappeared just as Jim arrived to drive me home. She smiled and hugged me warmly, and I inhaled her aroma of soap and spices, and something else... something unfamiliar, but very appealing. Her small, dense breasts and rock-hard nipples pressed against my chest, and her strong arms enveloped me.

"Thank you so much." I said softly, hugging her back. "That was the absolutely best massage I've ever had."

I left, still bathed in afterglow, holding a business card with Don's name and phone number printed on it. "Call me," was written in pencil on the back of the card.

"Full... body... massage...!" I told Jim in the car, flinging my arms around him. "You were so right about this evening—it *was* a surprise and *just* what I needed!

But how did you know I'd go for it? Or that she would?"

"I didn't." he said, looking pleased with himself as we left the Castro and headed for my neighborhood. "But I knew Don favored petite, curvy, dark-haired women with full breasts—and that you, my sweet, were horny enough to be up for anything. And I thought, *maybe, just maybe,* you weren't the straight little arrow you think you are." Jim arched his brows and flashed me a smug grin. "I planned it so the opportunity was there."

Back at home, I gazed at Don's card for a long minute, recalling her strong, knowing fingers and hot, wet mouth, and the generous gift of pleasure she'd given me. But I hesitated, realizing that this erotic encounter had awakened something in me I hadn't known was there.

If I met with her again, it would only be right to return the favor.

How would that be, I wondered, to have *her* spread out naked on her own massage table, looking up at me the way I'd looked up at her, quivering with anticipation? What would it be like for me: bending to kiss her moist, fragrant opening; parting her labia and lapping at her engorged clit with my tongue; while penetrating her with my fingers, kneading, massaging and delighting her... until she begged to be finished off?

And what sort of lover would I be? Would I know instinctively how to please her because we're both women? Or would I depend on her to guide me through it? How would it feel if I called her? To hear her low, husky voice on the phone and hear myself say, "Don, I'd *love* to see you again."

Heart thumping in my chest, I took a deep breath and called the number. As Jim said, the opportunity was there.

The tongue is a source of pleasure in so many ways, isn't it? This next poem by Rose Mark is an *amuse bouche* for your mind.

Rose K. Mark

MY CUNNING LINGUIST

My cunning linguist can
Twist, slide, poke,
Stretch, titillate,

His tongue can
Dart like a lizard
To a Zydeco beat,

quick quick, slow,
quick quick slow
quick quick slow

oh, oh, oh,
GO!

lick
flick
slick
stride

curl
soothe
schmooze

Oh so smooth

Prime my rind
swab my deck
Give a grand sweep

Make me sweat,
Plane my landing strip
My engines running
Squirming
I'm ready for takeoff!
Whooooo, ooooooooo Wheeeeeee!

J Mork is the pseudonym of a multitalented woman who got a degree in ceramics and promptly realized full-time ceramics jobs were not available. Her dramatic ability led her into her life's real vocation: sex work. Her writing reflects her fifteen years of experience as a sex worker in the Bay Area. As a person who has had cancer, she also investigates how Western medicine systems and ideologies intersect with human sexuality. Mork says she loves to travel and claims the ability to make any hotel an erotic wonderland – or a writing retreat.

This story is a fascinating, fly-on-the-wall look at the way sex work can be both work and, if you're up for it, sex at the same time.

THE FOURTEENTH HOUR

On the fourteenth straight hour of the toe-sucking session, I give in. We've been in this room for fourteen hours, with variations of me rolling around on his king-size bed with my feet dangling over the side. I've watched Brazilian trans porn with him since 6:30 p.m. I wonder if I'm a bad person for enabling this coked-out bender – or should I blame the toes that he obsesses over?

I realize he has been doing this for his entire lifetime, and I am just his most stable toe hussy. I really only exist as toes to him, yet he often mentions how close he feels to me. I don't judge him and keep him entertained with no residual, real-life consequences.

For these sessions, I arrive on time with snacks, magazines and cans of cold coffee. I have perfectly pedicured toes with no open skin. My middle-aged feet are still soft, the arches high and firm. My toes are painted an opaque, 1960s white. I plan my footwear all week to make sure that I have no besmirched skin.

But here I am at the fourteenth hour of silent porn, and I am really getting antsy. I realize I'm holding myself so still inside that I'm disappearing.

My eyes go to the all-porn TV. I notice my latest porn selections have been downloaded. In our years together, we have gone from VHS to DVD to downloading. Abstracted, overlapping hours marked by tech upgrades.

I start thinking, why don't I get off? So what if I cum and he doesn't? I didn't do coke all night, so my clit is still very alive. My hands start wandering around the bed – the bed covered in shoes, nude nylons and leg show magazines encrusted with aged lube. I creep my hands into my ho bag to extract wet wipes. My hands are filthy by this time, so I clean them carefully, knowing that touching oneself safely is safer sex too. I start stroking myself, supplying the missing onscreen dialogue with more intimately targeted storylines.

I start circling into myself, and he begins to look concerned, but the coke in his nose prevents his words from leaving his brain. He watches me play with myself, still silently rubbing his nylon-tied, lube-slimed genitals.

I cum in a gushing torrent and settle back down in a pile of womanly clutter. I think of the judgments I has always held on myself for denying myself pleasure before this session. What had I been waiting for? His expression of concern for my sexual self?

I pull a pot cookie out of my bag and take a bite, showing him with my placid calmness that just because I cum doesn't mean I'm going to leave. It's just that, after fourteen hours of porn, I needed some self-soothing stimulation at my own hands, which were not as busy as my toes.

The multi-talented Anita Placebo has written an erotic cookbook and held pussy-casting workshops. She wrote this story especially for Dirty Old Women. It's a cheeky, good-hearted satire of a certain stereotype of the ex-hippie chick.

When asked for a bio, she responded, "Anita Placebo's dreams come true. She delights in nature, the smell of your body and your loving touch. She is a dedicated student of Human Relationship, Body Language and Metaphysics." Hmmm, maybe this story isn't a satire at all.

Anita Placebo

PSYCHIC PUSSY

I usually start work around 11 a.m. or noon – or, if I need to recharge my spiritual batteries, one or two in the afternoon.

Starting my work day means walking the garden path from my sweet cottage tucked in among the draping jasmine and creaky eucalyptus to the storefront at the front of the property. My storefront. Once Albert's Staples and Sundries established 1924, but since 1974 and my purple paint job, Madame Jackson, Royal Psychic.

I never lock the door to the shop. Robbers stopped dropping by years ago, after I started leaving them treats on the stoop like cupcakes, roses, and love letters channeled from Mother Isis: "Dear Thief, Take everything that is yours."

I live on Alcatraz, such a busy street, I used to fret to myself. The rush hour drone crinkled my aura and depleted my spirit in the early years of business. But since 1984, the year of my first visit to Ashland, Oregon, where I drank the lithium waters of Light, and learned the Ancient Draper's Enchantment, I insulate my entire property from the din with a heavy opaque velvet aura and have enjoyed twenty years of peaceful city living since then.

These days, customers get confused looking for my shop. They want to know if it's in Berkeley or Oakland, what should they tell their computer phones when they ask it for directions? I say, "Follow your Intuition, it will always lead you where you need to go, and that's usually back to me." The neon sign helps, too.

Okay, so who is my first client of the day? The appointment book is empty, as always, because people typically show up exactly at the time that's right for them anyway. I begin preparing my body by getting naked, checking in with my chakras, stroking my ether body, massaging my third eye open, scanning the world for patches of human-shaped light making their tender way towards me. The doorbell jangles, and business walks in.

It's John. John brings neither relief nor disappointment, but rather an ecstatic rush of YAY! John is one of my favorite customers, and psychics are definitely allowed to have favorites. His dilemmas are clean and innocent, and he's always open to the power of my suggestion.

Should he vacation in The Bermuda Triangle, or Transylvania? Actually, the spirits tell me, Zanzibar. Would his mother prefer gardenias or roses? Both! She's 101 this year!! What should he name his new kitten? Jesus, because he's definitely a fickle kitty.

I'm so excited for our session to begin, and I can tell he is, too, because his pants are already bulging at the zipper. Our routine is familiar, but it certainly hasn't gone stale. I lounge on my chaise, my energy field buzzing and awakened, as he stands inches away from my face and frees his dick from those tight, chafing jeans, the same style and cut he wore during his stint in the Outback, and I swear they still smell like horse and saddle.

I begin to focus my psychic powers, honing in on the beam of light emanating from the tip of his dick, because that's where all the answers will come from. John begins slowly jerking off, because he knows I need to study his dick before it will begin talking to me, before I can receive any information at all. I take note of his precum – sparkling clear jewels flowing swiftly and steadily and stringing into a silver thread before dancing to the floor in a plop. There's a lot of it today, he must be well hydrated, doing an excellent job of paying respect to the holy sprites of the electrolytes, fostering connection to the fluid and endless flow of life and abundance by drinking lots of water.

He hasn't asked me his question yet, but I can already feel the answer beginning to take shape in my pussy.

I invite him down to my couch by kneeling on it, my ass turning to face him. He's really excited to get his answers, and I'm really excited to find out what they are, so we eagerly press our bodies together.

His dick and hips squeeze up next to my upturned ass, and tingles of electricity fly across our skin where it touches. With each slow and steady stroke, every square millimeter of his dick makes deliberate communication with the receptive skin inside my vagina.

I was fourteen when I learned about the psychic power of my pussy. It was September 1957, the month of my first ovulation, and I found myself making out with my best friend in a tree after school. We were wedged between its massive trunk and a thick generous branch, and, as her fingers slipped inside my young, eager body, a pussy-mind-connection exploded inside me with brightly-lit visions. My ears rang with a truth I could not keep inside: "You, Madeline Onker, will one day win one million dollars."

And she did, ten years later, as the youngest Nobel laureate in the field of Transliminal Intergender Metaphysics in 1967.

But John – and the visions he is giving me! As the friction between his cock and my psychic pussy intensifies, I see a scene of inspiring beauty. He is captain of a sailboat whisking over turquoise water in a warm tropical breeze. His skin glows under the sunset sun, and The Ocean World dances beneath his ship. Dolphins nip at the spray streaming off the bow, giant tortoises swim slowly below, rainbow coral and schools of neon fish coexist happily beneath his vessel.

I can feel his dick harden even more inside me, his pounding pace increases, and the inside of my body rushes to open, creating a magnificent pleasure space for his final, glorious Transmission. He starts to cum, buckets of his saltwater cum filling my happy working girl's pussy. I clamp my muscles shut, so I can absorb every last globule of information his spirit body is sharing with mine.

"YES!" I gasp in ecstasy, "You should DEFINITELY BUY THE SAILBOAT!"

He pays me for my orgasm and promptly renames the boat after me.

All in a day's work for a seventy-four-year-old psychic and her bright neon sign.

The many-faceted Jan Steckel is the author of the fiction chapbook *Mixing Tracks* (Gertrude Press, 2009) and poetry chapbook *The Underwater Hospital* (Zeitgeist Press, 2006). From her home in Oakland, she delights us with poetry, fiction and creative nonfiction. This poem shows that, in the right hands, even our electronic gizmos can be earthy and soulful.

Jan Steckel

WHY YOU DON'T WANT TO BORROW MY LAPTOP

A fine poet searched for a compliment,
said he loved the way I wrote about sex.
I'll tell you my secret: my husband
falls asleep earlier than I do.

At night in bed, I cup his balls
in my hand and cuddle,
talk pillow talk, good night,
sleep tight, sweet dreams.

My hand smells great afterward,
my own secret aromatic bouquet.
I get up and type for a couple of hours,
spread cock and balls all over the keyboard.

Chris Orr is a writer, cybrarian and bicyclist who lives right on the Oakland/Berkeley border. She says this borderline existence keeps her mindful of the dual nature of existence as material and spirit. That sense of duality is reflected in this dreamy tale of two women stuck in that most liminal of spaces, an airport. If only my next flight could begin like this.

Chris Orr

TO JOANI

I was in the airport when I read the news about the death of Joani Blank. Joani! Now there was a light gone from the world. She was seventy-nine—a pretty good run. She gave us so much in terms of pleasure, self-expression and feminism way back when she founded the Good Vibrations store. We knew it was a revolutionary act to sell sex toys to women in a clean, well-lighted place.

In Joani's honor and to pass the time until takeoff, I took a piece of paper out of my carry-on and made a list of my sex toys. At first, all I could think of were the small things: nipple clamps, a purple blindfold, ben wa balls, a very clever pair of suction nipple cups you press on and pull to create a tender vacuum. My list grew with larger things: fur-lined handcuffs with shiny links, crafty homemade floggers I made from bike inner tubes, the trusty old-school Hitachi wand with a detachable silicone tickler, the ball gag with long pink straps, a harness with velvet thongs and adjustable dildo ring.

I looked around at the people waiting near my gate and imagined what sex toy was packed in their bags for their travels. The trouble was, there was no erotic energy in the airport. Everyone seemed to be in stress mode, like the irate couple bickering over there about travel details

(I'd give them the flogger), and the hassled parents trying to corral kids (handcuffs, definitely). Then I saw this one redeeming thing.

At the end of the concourse, a huge picture window overlooked an estuary. Not the runway, this was a view of nature—an expansive view of our rainy day shower. I could gaze through that window and see miles to the horizon where water met sky. Out there, I saw a crease of pink in the sky with a slight blooming of deeper rose above it. The hidden sun blushed the clouds in that faraway place.

I stood still, enthralled by the veil of rain below the glower of clouds, the estuary all shiny grays fringed by green pampas grass on the shore close to the windows. I felt someone near me – a woman, standing and looking at the view with me.

"Beautiful isn't it?" she said.

She was dressed in a pale yellow jacket, soft knit, zipped up the front, and tailored black slacks. Her hair was tied back in a loose ponytail with a tortoiseshell barrette, no makeup on her handsome face, full lips, smiling. She pointed her chin at the view then turned her head toward me, her hands holding the strap of her bag across her shoulder and breasts. She looked to be in her fifties, with an air of mature dignity and self-possession that attracted me. I was a little astonished at seeing her next to me in this quiet moment, contemplating nature from within the cacophony of airport announcements and crowds. All of that faded to a background buzz with just her couple of words coming through, murmured into my ear.

Our backs to the terminal bustle, we watched a cormorant fly across our view. It entered the water, floated to the bank and stepped onto land to spread and dry its wings before taking off again, its darker silvers and grays etched against the estuary.

We gasped together, enjoying the moment of synchronicity. We were happy to witness the beautiful dance, a show of nature for those of us trapped indoors at the airport.

I took some more peeks at my companion, trying to be surreptitious, but she caught me. I blushed, because I was matching her with one of my sex toys. I pictured the clever ball gag with the small dildo attached to it. Frankly, I bought it on a whim and still wondered how it worked. I thought she would look good crouching in front of me to show me, eyes smiling, her intent serious.

She turned and said our flight was delayed an hour, did I know? And, would I like to join her in the airline lounge with hot drinks till we were called back to our gate?

My legs wobbled at the luck of it. The lounge was right there and opened with a swipe of her card. It was like a private reading room, deep cushioned armchairs and love-seats, wide and comfortable. There was a small self-service bar with one of those European machines that makes fresh coffee, hot chocolate and espresso drinks at the press of a button. Or did I prefer one of the teas in the wooden humidor on the bar? I flicked through the box while she claimed a couple of window seats facing the same view we had from the waiting room. A row of potted ficus plants screened our seats from the room.

I walked over with my steaming tea. She welcomed me and walked away to get her own drink. When she returned, she reached past me to set her cup on the small table next to my chair, and then knelt at my feet. Another surprise, she placed both her hands on my knees and gently drew them apart, moving one hand to rest warmly on my pussy, cupping the junction just so with her thumb curling under the crease of my thigh. I let out a sigh, careful not to be too loud and break the spell.

She moved in closer and breathed hot into the seam, then lifted herself up to replace her hand with her thigh, her knee resting on the edge of my chair close to my body so she could lean into me more fully as I spread my legs wider and lifted my hips to meet her.

We kissed like this, our bodies touching, her hands braced against the back of my chair. We were hungry girls, not having exchanged more than a few sentences, but aware of our need to taste our lips and tongues, get to know each other wordlessly this way, communicating fully clothed but intimate. I grasped her ponytail and pulled her head back to look into her eyes, just checking to see if she was ok and also to let her know I was in the verge of coming. No words, just my eyes looking into hers with the fluency of desire.

She shifted onto my chair, her legs straddling me now. I pulled my legs a little closer to accommodate her on the cushion. I unzipped her trousers and slipped my hands into the space where my thumbs could reach in to massage her fur and clit beneath.

She cuddled her face into my neck, breathing into my ear, rocking her hips to give me more access, her scent rising to me, a warm, fresh sea smell that blended with the beauty of the view over her shoulder.

Until now we had been miraculously alone in the lounge, screened by the row of plants. But we heard the door release as someone else swiped a card for entry. We leaned away from each other, reluctant to end our embrace.

Some orgasms take a while to build and crest, some peak up and down in a fierce quickness. We looked at each other and simultaneously chose the latter. It was the same as the stripe of clouds: beautiful pink, then swollen gray, then a veil of rain coming down.

Very soon after, she stood with a great deal of grace and a smile. We adjusted our clothes and returned to our hot drinks.

Lifting her cup, "To Joani," she said.

Donna George Storey aims to arouse our minds as well as our libidos with her erotica. She says, "The erotic experience is one of the most challenging and important parts of human existence to capture in prose. I truly believe we need more writers willing to acknowledge that the sexual urge and the erotic imagination are as worthy of a complex literary treatment as anger, jealousy, ambition, or love in its PG-rated form." Unlike many writers of erotica, she publishes mainstream fiction under the same name, and she's received a couple of nominations for the Pushcart Prize. The following story, written especially for this collection, is a fervent exploration of the mind as erogenous zone.

ORGASM ROAD

"Ladies, it's official. Sam and I have opened up our marriage."

Jenny had been talking about this particular solution to her "lust problem" for a number of years, so neither Jill nor I should have been particularly surprised. But we were.

"So, uh, what does that mean exactly?" Jill managed to say. I was still picking my jaw up off the floor.

"It means I've been very busy over the last four months. Have I got some stories to tell you!"

When I invited Jill and Jenny over for a long-overdue reunion of our mother's group, I thought we'd compare notes on our kids' freshman year of high school and marvel over how quickly they'd grown. I'd even pulled out my photo albums from the old days, when the three of us gathered once a week at a local park to watch our first-borns attack the sand box with plastic shovels and scoot down the toddler slide on diapered bottoms.

Come to think of it, though, Jenny's announcement was as much a part of our history as shaking sand out of tiny shoes. Early on, she told us

Sam had lost interest in sex after Megan was born. Jill and I tried to assure her their sex life would revive soon—in fits and starts, perhaps, but in some ways it got better. We recommended date nights and get-away weekends, and all the other tips and tricks we'd read in magazines and tried ourselves. But Sam insisted he just wasn't feeling sexual, although he still regarded Jenny as his best friend.

If your partner isn't interested anymore, do you have to give up sex forever?

Jenny had apparently answered that question for herself at last.

I refilled our wine glasses. Pete was away on business and Sophie was sleeping over at a friend's. As far as I was concerned, Jenny could tell us scandalous stories all evening.

And she did.

Their agreement was this: The welfare of the children came first. She and Sam would still live together and co-parent, but they'd each have several evenings a week to go out on their own, no questions asked. Jenny went online and soon met a man who eased the road back to the dating scene. This man, Mark, helped her write a better profile to interest the kind of man she was looking for, told her about the happening dating sites, and slept with her twice a week for a month. The sex was mind-blowing, especially after years of drought, but Mark was committed to "an ongoing exploration of sensuality in its purest form." They still slept together every now and then, but he didn't have time for more.

Which was fine with Jenny, because she'd had a steady boyfriend for the last month. He was twenty-seven.

"He's twenty years younger than you?" I gasped. Jenny was the youngster of the group. Jill and I had both celebrated our fiftieth birthdays in the past year.

"Now, what's that like?" Jill asked evenly, always the model of tact. What I wanted to ask is: *Does he fuck you all night?*

"Kevin likes to go dancing, so we usually go to a club and then back to his place. The sex is great. Kevin says he loves being with an older woman, a woman who knows what she wants. He says women his own age aren't nearly as responsive. Plus they're so into defining the relationship. With me, it's all about the fun and the sensuality."

"I haven't gone out to a club in twenty-five years," Jill said with a chuckle. "By ten o'clock, I'm in my jammies and ready for bed."

"Oh, you'd be surprised how quickly you get back in the swing of it. The other night I hit it off with a guy I met at a dance club. He's from Rome, absolutely gorgeous. Just twelve years younger, but still. We haven't slept together yet, but he sends me suggestive texts in Italian. I'm learning a lot of new words."

So Jenny was getting a linguistic education in the bargain. What wasn't to applaud? Still, it must be strange to make such a big change in your life.

Jenny smiled, as if she'd read my thoughts. "Listen, you two. I'm not sure what you're really thinking about all this, but I love being wanted again. It's amazing. From the very first night I put up my profile, I started getting emails from guys complimenting me, courting me. You might consider going online and joining one of these sites. You don't have to go any farther, but the attention you get will make you feel pretty and sexy and very alive."

My old friend certainly looked happier than she had in years. In fact she positively glowed.

Before we knew it, it was midnight, and Jill's husband arrived to take my guests home so they didn't have to drive under the influence. I saw them off with a cheerful wave and a mutual promise to do this again soon. It only occurred to me afterwards that, unlike for Jill and me, a mother's group reunion would no longer be a big night out for Jenny.

Singles bars, erotic tutoring by a libertine, dancing-in-the-sheets with a grateful young man. For her, the possibilities were limitless.

It was one o'clock by the time I'd loaded the dishwasher and got myself to bed. I missed Pete and Sophie, but I was glad, too, that I had time to process Jenny's news alone. I'd tried my best to be non-judgmental. God knows she deserved to have some fun. But the idea of going out after dark and sleeping with strangers, after decades of intimacy with one man, was troubling to me.

And, to be honest, arousing as hell.

I snuggled under the blankets, knowing that of course I was going to masturbate tonight, inspired by the things Jenny said—and even more by the things she didn't say.

Certainly, our situations were very different. Pete and I had had our challenges over the years. All married couples do. It took some time to get it right at the beginning. Pete was sometimes impatient with me and complained I "took too long." Being rather inexperienced himself, he didn't appreciate that when I came, it was for real. I'd sworn never to fake it again after my first relationship, when I did. My husband has since apologized for being an asshole—and learned to appreciate the slow road to pleasure himself. We still made it a point to have sex at least twice a week. My periods still came every twenty-eight days, but who knew how long we had left and what it would be like after menopause?

Pete was a master at pleasuring me now, but over the years I'd learned some things about myself, too. I knew it wasn't just my body but my mind that needed release from the land of reality, where good wives and mothers were always circumspect, where any female who gave the least sign of comfort with eroticism was fair game, where sex was a dangerous thing for a woman. I also knew a man didn't "give" me an orgasm. He and I took that path together, to a place where trust dissolves the rules, where bodies and minds entwine, where pleasure blossoms in the heat and sweat and blissful madness of it all.

Tonight I'd take my own little solo trip down Orgasm Road.

Without Pete's hands and lips and warmth, I needed heavy-duty fantasy to ignite the flame. No pretty romantic tales for me, no, Orgasm Road brought out my tough and dirty side.

I slipped my hand under my pajama pants and stroked myself gently.

The journey had begun.

How about that Mark character? Jenny's tutor in Promiscuity 101. I hated his kind. A man who doesn't let anything stand in the way of his selfish desires. Everyone knows that playboy facade masks sex addiction and a phobia of intimacy. I'm sure he loved to take an inexperienced polyamorist under his wing to show her the tricks.

Teach me, Mark. You teach me, and I'll teach you something, too.

My finger moved faster. I squeezed my pussy muscles rhythmically to bring on a nice sexual buzz in my belly.

How did these things happen nowadays? You meet the first time at a Starbucks or something. A safe, public, place. You check each other out and go your separate ways if you don't click. But Mark and I linger over our lattes. He's handsome, obviously. He wouldn't get so many women to go along with his agenda if he wasn't. Early fifties, toned body, salt-and-pepper hair, a sexy gaze that promises a woman everything, if only for one night.

I can tell from the light in his eyes that he likes me. He knows I have something up my sleeve. A man like him thrives on challenge.

He suggests we go to a cocktail lounge where we can talk more freely. In a dark corner booth, he tells me I'm a beautiful, sexy woman, and it would be an honor to give me pleasure. Within the hour, we agree to go to a nearby motel together. Why not? There's no need to pretend we wanted anything else from each other.

He gallantly stands aside to let me enter the room first. There's a king bed, a small sofa, a desk, a

TV screen mounted on the wall. All useless to us, except the bed. I turn and face him. He smiles and takes me in his arms. He tells me again that I'm beautiful and he looks forward to exploring sensuality in its purest form with me.

Sure, Mark, I want to fuck you, too, without knowing very much about you except your cock is hard and your fingers tireless. But I don't say that. Yet.

We kiss. He kisses well, which means he takes it slow. A kiss, I suppose, means this isn't a commercial transaction. No, we're two mature adults exploring our natural human need for variety outside the stifling institution of marriage. We do this with the full consent of our spouses. Or so he tells me, and my spouse, well, of course, we worked it out somehow–at this point in the fantasy, that's a minor point.

Bathed in the dim light filtering through the motel curtains, Mark and I keep kissing, tasting the foreign flavors of each other. He pulls me closer and I feel his erection. It's a nice size, from what I can tell. I do want to fuck this man. He smells right, his touch is assured, and as Jenny told us, in this game you are forthcoming about your needs. The men like it that way. They want to know how to please you. And if they don't do it right, you get up and walk away.

Mark asks if he can undress me. I'm in decent shape for my age, the light is low. Why not? His hands are hot and his breath quickens as he unwraps me eagerly, like a birthday present. *Lovely*, he whispers. I reach for the buttons of his shirt, fumbling in my haste. I want him naked, too. His chest is nice. I can tell he works out—a requirement for his recreational tastes, no doubt—even if his flesh is mellow-soft with age. He unbuckles his belt and removes trousers while I watch. Shapely legs, pubic hair light brown—or is it mixed with gray? His cock is already hard, honoring me with a perpendicular middle-aged salute. It's thick and hefty but not too long. Just the way I like it.

We crawl under the hotel quilt and slide over the sheets into an embrace. He pushes his thigh between mine and I rub my slit against him, smearing him with my female juices. Then he takes my nipple between his lips—under my own blankets I tweak my own nipple with my free hand–and he rubs my clit, his finger finding the groove a little to the right, where it's most sensitive.

He strums patiently until I'm squirming and the sheets are damp from the sweat of our bodies. I tell him I want him inside me. Now. He rolls on a condom and lies back to let me straddle him, because I mentioned in the cocktail lounge that I come more reliably that way. He watches as I slide onto him, fascinated by the sight of two strangers joining in the most intimate connection. I take him in to the hilt, then rest there, adjusting my legs so my clit presses against his belly.

He has, by the old reckoning, had his way with me.

Now I'll have *my* way with him.

Murmuring, taunting, teasing him with my words, I hold him captive between my thighs while I milk his cock with my secret muscles.

I'm going to fuck you, now, Mark. I'm going to fuck you my way. Is that all right?

A smile plays over his lips. He nods.

You can't come until I say so. Do you understand?

My tone is sweet, but the flicker in his eyes— fear mixed with arousal–shows he knows I mean business. Does he like to be taken in hand by a strong woman? Maybe they all do.

I begin to grind against him, rocking my hips just enough to please myself.

So you've scored another pussy to add to your long list of conquests, Mark, you insatiable sex addict who can never be happy with one woman. But I have a new rule for you. You can't count our little tryst if you don't please me. In fact, you'll lose all your pussy points and go straight back to zero as if you've never known a woman in your life. So you'd better do it right, Mark. Listen well. I want you to rub my asshole now, tease it with your thick finger. My asshole is as responsive as my clit. My husband and I figured that out after years of playing in bed, but I'm sharing my special secret with

*you just hours after we first laid eyes on each other.
Aren't you a lucky man?*

He moans assent, as his hand glides down and around to cradle my ass. A finger slips between the crack. Obediently he circles the tender pink opening.

Now don't try to go inside. No finger-fucking for a serial bad boy like you. Just stroke the outside very gently like a good boy.

He sighs.

Oh, yeah, that's good, Mark. You tease my butt hole while I squeeze you like a milking machine. I exercise my cunt, Mark. I train my body and make my muscles strong because I like sex as much as you. Later, when you're scanning profiles for your next girlfriend of the afternoon, remember how hard I grip you while you tickle my anus and suck my nipples. Remember how I tell you exactly what I want from you. You like that, don't you? A woman who tells you exactly how to drive her wild?

Yes, he whispers, *yes, I do.*

Well, I'll tell you what you have to do for this hotel encounter to count on your precious fuck tally. I'm never satisfied with one man either. After I come on your cock, I'll need more orgasms, lots more. So once I'm finished, you'll hop right out of bed with your aching boner and get me some nice young men with your savvy internet one-time-fuck-finding talents. You like to help women get laid, don't you, Mark? Today I want a couple of horny guys, twenty-five to thirty years old. Big, healthy fellows with thick cocks.

I'll get them for you, he murmurs, his eyes closed as if enduring a sweet pain. *I'll do anything you say.*

I'm moving faster on top of him. This clit-and-ass stimulation is working like a charm.

I'll show them what a real woman wants. One will kiss my breasts while the other eats my pussy until I'm ready. Then I'll pick which one gets to fuck my tight, horny asshole while the other rubs my clit until I come. But it won't be you, Mark. I want you to sit in that chair in the corner and watch us enjoying our sensuality in its purest form. Maybe if you're good, though, I'll let you play with yourself. But you can't come until both of those strong young things have shot their loads into me. And then, just maybe, I'll give you permission to come in your own hand.

God, I'm being such a bitch, but that humiliating scene seems to turn old Mark on something fierce. He groans and leans up to take my nipple in his hot, wet mouth as if he's starving for it.

I wet my own fingers and flick my nipple hard and fast. My ass is bucking on the mattress as the tension builds in my belly. Oh, I'm close, so close, lost in that crazy place where everything is twisted together. I'm the severe mistress, giving my lover what he wants, even if he's never known he wanted it until this moment. And I'm the insatiable bad boy, aching with frustration but reveling in it, my fear of missing out on life's endless orgy exposed before her knowing eyes.

I'll show her. I'll come in her cunt before she can stop me. She wants it, why else would she squeeze my cock like a fist? God, her asshole's the key to the kingdom. Her cunt's been gushing from the moment I touched it. She seemed so self-possessed in the coffee shop, appraising me with her cool gaze as if I wasn't good enough for her. I love to see them come undone, the way they writhe and wriggle when they're impaled on my dick. She's gonna come soon, yeah. I feel it in that desperate, syncopated thrust of her hips. She's groaning like an animal and, to hell with her bitchy orders, I'm gonna plunge my finger deep in her ass and yeah, now she's screaming in ecstasy and I'm coming, too, shooting up into her, I'm coming, coming, coming....

With a long, low moan, I ride to the finish on Orgasm Road.

I lie back with a smile and feel my heartbeat slow to normal.

That was a good one. Really good for a solo run. I do miss Pete. There's nothing like floating in his arms after we make love, the most satisfying feeling in the whole world. But I feel pretty damn good, now, too.

The afterglow makes me generous. I wish them all well on their chosen path, my muses of the evening. I'm glad Jenny finally feels desired. I hope Mark's partners are having fun, too, as he pursues his endless quest. And Sam–perhaps the change will help him figure out what he wants, too.

Relaxed and sated, I know I'll sleep well tonight. A trip along Orgasm Road always brings you home.

By now, you've gotten to know the wicked, witty wordsmith who is Jan Steckel. I'll just add that she's an activist in the bisexual community and an advocate on behalf of the disabled and the underprivileged. Now, get ready for a tongue-twister. In fact, for the full effect, I suggest you read this with your mouth pressed to someone else's nether mouth or member.

Jun Steckel

MAKE-UP SEX

Post-tiff, still miffed,
my quim has a whim for him
though he looks grim.
He's quite stiff (though gruff)
for a whiff of my quiff
a sniff of my muff.

Let's play a sweet riff
while smoking a spliff.
He'll strut his stuff, get tough.
He's buff, no bluff.
Okay, okay, I'm ready
to fluff the duffer.

Beth Elliott is a multi-generation California native, with a Tidewater Virginia heritage and a Jesuit education. In other words, she warns, be extremely afraid. Beth recently told me, "Scintillating, risqué and bizarre are right in my wheelhouse." I'd say so. This sweet and melancholy story is a very modern take on a folkloric theme.

ZOE HOWARD

Nobody knew about Zoe Howard and me, and that's a fact. If anybody had noticed anything, they would have said something. Nobody ever notices anything different about me, so it's almost like she'd never even been here. But I remember Zoe Howard. And sometimes I think about Zoe Howard and me.

I met her in the park late one night. I know that sounds kind of weird, but I work the swing shift at the chip fabrication plant they moved in here a few years back. And it was around my daughter's birthday, the baby I put up for adoption after the high school sweetheart who always talked about being in love forever got me pregnant and skipped town. I was feeling kind of blue, like I get, and wondering if that would pass or sneak up and hit me like it did that year when she would have been the same age as I was when I had her.

So I wasn't really in the mood to go straight home and decide whether to take out those few baby pictures and stare at them or leave them tucked away. It had been a while since I'd had to fend off questions at work about photos of my own with, "Always a bridesmaid, never a grandmother," but the "never a bride" thing was something else I didn't want jumping up and biting me.

I recognized her at once; she was that pale, skinny-looking thing from the mini-mart where I stop on the way home sometimes. She was wearing this cape and acting all mysterious like she wanted to scare me or something, until I said, "Oh, please, I'm really not up for playing Creature Features, and this isn't the drive-in anyway."

She looked startled, then confused, then kind of relieved. "You are not afraid of being alone out here in the dark?" she asked. "Who knows who could be lurking out here? Muggers ... rapists ... or," and she did some twirly thing with her cape, "children of the night!"

"Number one," I said, "it's just the town park. I walk through here on my way home all the time. Number two, it's not like I'm some kind of hot mama or any other weirdo bait. I don't see myself running into anything more exotic than some drunken hobo, and I think I can deal with one of them. Number three, I'm just a hometown girl stuck working swing shift at the chip plant. Any children of the night who caught up with me would be bored silly in two minutes."

"Then ... then you are ... but you seem too world-weary to be just ... ordinary."

"Well, you're wrong there, cause I'm about as ordinary as they get, unless you want to count all the girls like me who actually got to get married before not living happily ever after."

"You are ordinary, and yet I do not frighten you. Or intrigue you." She sighed a long, tired sigh, but instead of looking disappointed, she seemed pretty pleased with herself. "I knew it could happen. I told them they were wrong."

That remark kind of puzzled me. This was not your regular oddball-type behavior. But she looked like someone in need of a friend, not because she was lonely in particular, but because she was so odd. Here in Texas people make distinctions between eccentric and odd, and odd isn't looked upon nearly as kindly. So I did what should come next and introduced myself.

"Delighted to make your acquaintance, Rosalie McFall," she replied. Then she took my hand and kissed it, of all things, and said, "I am Zoe Howard," as though I'd asked her if she was. Then she said, "The night is so inspiring. Please allow me to entertain you with a story." And she did. It was a ghost story; a really good one, too. I told her she should write books like Stephen King, cause she could probably make a whole lot of money at it.

"Stephen King?" she said, all indignant. "Ha! He knows nothing!"

I laughed at that and told her she was a hoot.

Anyway, I started hanging out with her, after she'd close up the mini-mart. I'd catch a nap after my shift, then pick up a snack on our way to the park. Sometimes I'd brown-bag something so I wouldn't keep eating all that fast food, but I never saw her eat a thing. But every night she'd tell me a different story, and every one a good one, too. Then she got into acting them out as she told them. I don't remember when her stories all started having her as a main character, or when I realized she really believed the stories she was telling.

Eventually I asked her, if she was this vampire, with these exotic friends and adventures and all, what was she doing working nights at a mini-mart out here in West Nowhere, Texas instead of hanging out in some castle somewhere. And for the first time, she lost that dramatic way of acting she had with me and looked like she was going to cry, only her eyes didn't even moisten.

"Ah, my dear Rosalie," she said, "that is the saddest story of all. I long so to tell you. But I must not. To tell you that story, I would have to ask something of you that I desire more than anything. Yet in my high regard for you, I dare not beg you to take that risk for me."

That's when I thought I had it figured out. Those stories about overcoming young maidens with only her seductive charm until they let her open their bodices, and what their letting her drink their blood really meant.

"Zoe Howard," I asked, "are you a lesbian or something?"

And maybe I expected her to be startled or guilty or something; I didn't understand her just looking confused. So I blurted out, "I don't mind, and I like you, and if you asked me I'd take you home and let you touch me and all.

Lord knows you're the only one in this town who treats me like I'm any kind of special, and I don't want to give up and expect nobody to ever make love to me again.

"But I don't have what it takes to live some exotic life like in the stories you tell me. I'm a plain ol' girl with a plain ol' job and a plain ol' life, and that's all I've got it in me to be. I was born ordinary, I'm ordinary now, and I'll die ordinary. If you want me for a girlfriend, Zoe Howard, I'll be that for you. But ordinary's all you'll get; I don't have what it takes to be different, to be a lesbian."

"I know," she said, real soft-like. "That is why you are beautiful to me. You love my stories, but are not in the least seduced by them. You are ordinary—and that is why I love you. And that is why you alone can bring me peace.

"My passion is indeed for women, my dear Rosalie. But it is not as a lesbian that I am honored by your friendship. No, it is not about that at all. I know I seem to you an aimless, affected youth with a fixation on vampires and other macabre lore. It has been centuries that I have been a youth, since I lost my only true love—a love for the ages—to a cruel and untimely illness. She was everything I was not; everything I wanted to become.

Inconsolable, I railed against the fate of all mortal flesh, and swore that the wound in my heart would never be healed without an immortal passion that could defy the grave.

"As one would do in that superstitious era, I studied what we ignorantly called the Black Arts. I haunted graveyards, doing foolish rituals and chanting silly backwards incantations. It was an accident that one of the undead found me before I caught my death from the chill and damp.

"I joined their company ecstatically, eager for a wedding of blood in which I could become one with a true love who could never be taken from me by death, whose youthful bloom I could preserve forever. I would not be denied that beloved Other who, by joining herself to me, would make me complete! But, accursed fool that I was, I failed to realize that, at the moment I transformed her into an immortal, she would cease to be anything but my creation. Again and again, I would look upon my bride and see not my counterpart, but only myself!

"And so I left the fantastical company of the undead to wander the ordinary places, seeking now only the end. The end! A desire my vampire instincts betray at every turn."

I shifted my weight to lean against her and rest my head on her shoulder. For the first time in my life, being ordinary no longer seemed something to quietly endure.

"Rosalie," she whispered, "I do not wish to ask you to take this risk, but I would beg of you one thing: take me home and keep me up till the dawn."

Till the dawn—I can't think of anything more romantic. I'd only been asked that once before—and by that dawn, I was pregnant. "Zoe Howard," I said, "isn't that kind of dangerous for a vampire?"

"It is for you, I fear, beloved friend," she replied.

She was right, too. I must have been out of my mind. For when she sucked on my breasts, I could feel teeth far too sharp to be human brushing either side of my nipples. She would alternately go into a frenzy—and I could almost swear she was growling deep in her throat—then get all quiet and still, touching me so gently I could hardly feel it. But wherever she touched me, each touch sent severe pleasure rippling through me.

I was an ocean in her hands, cresting and subsiding. At one point, when I'd come and come like never before in my life, she started to lose it. I saw the fangs and nearly panicked, especially because a part of me suddenly wondered with seductive curiosity what it would be like to feel the sharp pain in my breast and the warmth rushing out of my veins. Before I knew it, I'd wrestled her to the bed and had her pinned. Her eyes went wide, and a smile crossed her face—not her usual crooked grin, but an honest-to-God smile. And I don't know if I was just repeating things she'd done to me or what, but the way her body flowed at the command of my lips, tongue and fingers was astonishing ... I felt like I was flying.

I figured this would get us through till daylight, but that girl exhausted me. I lay on top of her for a moment to rest, and she got a second wind and was all over me again.

I knew her instinct would be to bite me before dawn. I could tell I was spent, but she was getting stronger and more passionate by the minute.

All I could do was trust her. And at one point, I found myself looking up into her eyes—her crazed eyes—and relaxing and smiling meekly, then lowering my gaze. I knew I was a goner; if she wanted to, she could usher me into an afterlife of never-ending nightmare. And of course she wanted to. I knew in my mind I was screwed, but I felt so very, very free.

She laughed wildly then and stroked my cheek. Suddenly she was holding me and caressing me and telling me how precious I was. And I lost it. It hit me how frightened I'd really been, and I started whimpering and everything. But Zoe Howard held me, and kissed my forehead and cheeks over and over, and kept telling me I was so sweet and special and beautiful.

"Zoe Howard," I said, "look. It's getting light out. I think the sun's about to come up."

She clenched her eyes shut, arched her back and sucked a sharp breath deep into her lungs. But then she slowly leaned back down and gently kissed me. With her lips still pressed to mine, she cocked her head toward the window, opened an eye and ...

All I can say about her being gone is that I have no doubt all of it was for the best. I'm an ordinary girl and could never be like Zoe Howard.

But one thing has changed. I used to feel cheated that I never got to be a bride. Now I know being a bride isn't about wearing a gown and pledging yourself to a man of your own and being the center of all your girlfriends' attention. It's about a moment in your life when you come into who you are, when you surrender to your own glory for the first time and everything seems so clear for one blissful moment you'll never forget, for one moment that's all the forever you'll ever need. I've been a bride. I spent that one night with Zoe Howard.

Sometimes I think about her, late at night. When I do, the earthy smell of her is in the air again for just a moment. When I do, I feel the grit of her dust on my lips.

Amy Butcher is a writer and illustrator, and author of the 2012, award-winning mystery novel *Paws for Consideration*. Look for her latest project, the soon-to-be-released, adult coloring book *Wonder Body*. In addition to these literary activities, Amy serves as a liminal guide. About this transformational work, she says, "Liminal is the threshold, the transitional experience between two different states, the grey area. It is often a space that is deeply uncomfortable, a part of the journey we rush to get through. Yet there is much richness in playing in the liminal, in taking in all that can be harvested from that uncomfortable uncertainty." In her story, a woman must push through this grey area in order to reopen herself to lust and love.

DISH GLOVES TO DIE FOR

Some say familiarity breeds contempt, but for Nana, familiarity bred complacency. My grandmother had lived in that same home for half a century, had turned away from the kitchen sink to cross that floor so many times that her body knew the exact geography of those soft linoleum tiles . . . intimately, deeply, and beyond conscious thought. Her foot knew, down to the nearest millimeter, what it would take to clear the bumps and lifting edges of the old tile.

She must have been tired—conserving energy by skimming her foot a hair closer to the dull, soft surface. When it had met the freshly lifted corner of tile, stretching in the summer heat, it was no match. Her foot had caught, she had fallen, and the indifferent linoleum had offered nothing to break her fall, shattering her hip on impact.

She'd lain there through the night, silent in her agony, until morning, when the pain had subsided enough for her to finally scream. The neighbors had come quickly, and then the ambulance, and then all of us. I had kept vigil at her bedside, the memories of a lifetime filling the silent hours.

I could remember my small girl's fascination with the feminine toolset on her dressing table—the silver hairbrush, the tri-partite mirror and the alabaster jar of face powder. If I had been good, very good, she would invite me to sit on the small stool facing the mirror while she stood behind me. First, she would rake the brush through my unruly hair, each long, slow stroke of the soft-bristled brush trailed by the smooth stroke of her hand. The she'd reach across to remove the lid of the powder jar. She'd shake the puff applicator against the sides of the bowl, a tiny cloud of powder erupting all around us. Watching our infinite reflections in the three-paneled mirror, she'd flourish the applicator lightly across each of my cheeks, only to finish with the slightest, lightest touch—a kiss—of powder on the tip of my nose.

Nana had loved me steadily, dutifully, but she had always loved me as if through white gloves. She'd hug me at a polite distance, kissing the air beside my cheek rather than the skin upon it. I'd learned to love her back in that same proper way, sharing the light brush of affection as if that was all that one might ever need. But now, sitting beside Nana in her hospital bed, I reached out and gently traced the outline of her cheekbone, using the same softness I remembered from the brush of that powder, hoping that my love might be a boon, might speak through my touch. I felt the heat of my body arc out through her increasingly pale, paper-thin skin.

We are not an emotive family in life. Nana was the matriarchal anchor of our family, though, and her death set everyone adrift. My mother sobbed uncharacteristically and inconsolably. My sisters alternated between tears and stunned silence, leaning their heads onto the burly shoulders of their husbands for support, pulling their children close to their bellies for comfort. I alone clung to the familial shores, maintaining the composure I thought Nana would have expected, holding the tears in abeyance until a more appropriate time. The problem was, Nana had never told me when that time might be.

"I understand," Mary said patiently, "but couldn't one of your sisters have helped, too?"

I eyed my girlfriend with building annoyance. "We've been over this! They have kids, we don't. It's my responsibility anyway: I'm the oldest. You know you don't have to come if you don't want to," I said, crossing my arms with more bravery than I felt.

Someone had to pack up Nana's house. The task was overwhelming, and I needed Mary's help. But ever since Nana had died, Mary's concern had felt like salt in an open wound. I needed her there, and I wanted her to leave me alone. I could feel Mary's patience thinning, a chilliness growing in the space between us.

"Whatever. Of course, I'll come," Mary said, throwing her hands up in concession, "I'll do my best to be helpful..." and under her breath, "... and stay out of your way."

Although we had worked diligently, it had taken the better part of four days to feel we'd made a dent in things. The detritus of a life was daunting. What to do with the seven socks waiting patiently in the sewing basket to be darned? And the dusty decanter of brandy, sediment deeply coating the crystal of its oval bottom, was clearly no longer fit for drinking. My sadness deepened with each find. The stacks of plastic containers were easy enough to recycle, but the well-loved keepsakes presented more of a challenge.

Then there were the other small discoveries that started to hint at a side of Nana I'd never known—like the carefully saved photo and love letter from "Roger," a man no one in our family had ever heard of. Each of these discoveries created a splinter of doubt in my mind about this woman who had been a fixture in my entire existence, splinters that stung as they slid down quickly into my imagination, the point of entry vanishing as quickly as they had been made.

And still, I hoarded my tears.

On the final day, Mary stayed upstairs—still steering clear of me—while I worked down in the kitchen. I filled the sink with hot, soapy water, preparing to wash what few treasures remained.

Stretching precariously from the top of a stool, I reached into the back of each cabinet, pulling out items that had been lost in the corners for decades. From one, a small wooden mousetrap, an open box of baking soda—incapable of absorbing one additional molecule of odor—and a single Oreo cookie with tiny tooth-marks crenellating its edge. On another, a black and yellow tin of *Chock Full 'O Nuts*, empty but for the plastic scoop, and an ancient, squat, blue tin of *Crisco*, half full, the plastic lid yellowed and brittle with age. I placed them all in a heap on the counter.

The three drawers by the kitchen sink held a different set of surprises. Tucked in the back of the left-most drawer was a well-worn pink apron with the words "Hot Mama!" glued in glitter across the front. It was so out of character for Nana that it was hard for me to imagine how she might come by it and why on earth she'd kept it. In the next, just some old pink packets of *Sweet'N Low* locked in mortal combat with double cubes of *Domino Sugar* still sporting their tight-folded paper uniforms. Finally, in the way back of the very last drawer: the gloves.

To call them simply "dishwashing gloves" would not do them justice. Yes, they were pink, and they were built of that strange marriage of fabric on the inside and latex on the outside that gives them that distinctive floppy structure. But they were so much more than that. Whereas a traditional *Playtex* glove would have been married to a short sleeve finished with a simply pinked edge, this one was an entirely different beast.

From the same functional glove extended a thick fluted tube like the pistil of a calla lily. The ridges running up its length gave the sleeve a stand-up rigidity that kept it firmly hiked up to the wearer's elbow. As if that wasn't enough, at the top of the pistil sprung a riot of pink latex petals—no function beyond decoration—blooming outwards in one final floppy flourish. These were not your regular dish gloves. No, these were dish gloves with attitude.

I slumped onto the stool, holding the gloves and apron in my lap, and stared. I was tired and struggling to reconcile the woman who had loved me with such formality with this woman, the one who had coveted these gloves. The splinter of doubt started to fester and itch. The only way to resolve this incongruity was to put myself in her shoes—or gloves—and try and feel what Nana might have felt. Perhaps I could find my way into her heart through my own body.

I slipped on the apron first. Nothing, no insight, just amusement as I looked down and read the words emblazoned upside down across my breasts. I decided that a friend of hers, maybe an old college chum, had given the apron as a joke-present on some milestone birthday. She'd kept it out of her affection for the friend rather than for the apron itself.

Next, the gloves. I held their floppy length before me in one hand and could feel a strange buzz emanating from them. They set off a sympathetic vibration inside me, animating a strange feeling that had been percolating since we'd arrived. Nana's face flashed through my mind, encouraging me to pull them on. I obeyed—and shivered despite the humid summer air.

To counter my chill, I plunged both hands into the hot soapy water in the sink. The heat of the water pressed inwards, confusing my forearms, making them both warm and dry simultaneously. The confusion spread throughout my body.

Upstairs in the attic, Mary had been pulling down the last of the steamer trunks holding Grandpapa's old clothes. He'd been dead for years, but Nana had kept everything neatly stored away, just in case he might waltz back in one day. She believed in him that way, loved him that deeply and that long that his mortality was virtually unimaginable.

Grandpapa had been a dandy and, evidently, Mary had discovered that they wore the same size. Unable to resist the beautiful tailoring, she came waltzing into the kitchen sporting a top hat and full set of tails.

"What do you think, my lady?" Mary offered grandly yet with a hint of caution, still trying to read my mood.

"Very handsome," I nodded, always appreciative of Mary's broad butch shoulders.

"I think you need a break from all this work. A night on the town, perhaps?" she bowed slowly, one arm crossing behind her back while the other doffed the top hat and swept it in a wide arc across the front of her body.

Another shiver scurried up my spine and back down. The buzz in the gloves increased. "I'm hardly dressed for the occasion," I said, chagrined, glancing down at the feisty pink apron covering my yellow sundress.

"Oh, but you are! You're even wearing your formal evening gloves," she countered, pointing to my remarkable pink find.

In response, and of their own accord, my arms lifted up, and I shimmied from the shoulders like a burlesque dancer spinning her pasties, the gloves making that particular rubber flapping sound familiar from flat tires and fetish parties.

"Sweet!" she nodded in approval.

I frowned at my own behavior.

"Allow me?" Mary said, her eyes peering deeply into my own as she extended her hand.

One pink latex glove gracefully offered itself in response. She captured my rubberized fingers and bent slowly to kiss the back of my hand.

"Mmm, *Calgon*, take me away!" she said, lips smacking over the soapy taste.

"This is silly. We've got work to do!" I said, as I struggled to retrieve my gloved hand from her grasp.

"You're right, we do!" Mary countered, holding firm. "Come here."

Mary backed towards the kitchen counter, pulling me with her.

"Come on!" I resisted. As Mary pulled me closer, the ancient odor of *Old Spice* on Grandpapa's jacket made him come alive. I shook my head, trying to dismiss the distracting memory, only to have Nana's face take his place. She smiled and urged me forward.

Mary could take me down, but not without a fight. I put both pink-gloved hands against her chest and pushed, but she used that energy to spin us around. Now she leaned her weight against my back, sandwiching us face-first into the counter. She pressed in hard and reached around under my arm, taking my chin in her hand. Her lips brushed against the back edge of my ear. My neck arched back towards her in involuntary response as I felt her fingers wrap lightly around my throat.

"Imagine that it's Thanksgiving . . . many, many years ago," she whispered. "There's still so much work to be done: green beans to be snapped, potatoes to be mashed, and most important, a turkey to be stuffed." My mouth began to water at the images. "You do like stuffing, don't you?" She moved my jaw up and down.

"Yes . . . especially yours?" I offered tentatively through clenched teeth, still trying to figure out the rules of the game we were playing.

"Oh, but you're confused, my dear. You didn't think I was going to do the stuffing, did you?" When I hesitated, Mary forced my head left and right until I gave in, and the gesture became my own. "I may be well-dressed, but I'm also here to *be* dressed. These tails are turkey tails, baby!" Mary must have felt my frown of confusion. "I'll make it simple," she said, leaning in close. "Repeat after me."

I nodded.

She fed me the line, "Mary is my turkey, and she needs to be stuffed."

I started to shake my head no, but her grip tightened against my jaw. I could feel her need in the silence. I swallowed hard before repeating back the words.

Mary scanned the counter, her eyes landing upon the *Crisco*. She placed it squarely on the kitchen stool and flipped off the lid. Small flecks of rust from the rim had fallen into the silken white fat, streaking it dirty red. Grabbing both my arms, she swung me around so that now I was leaning against her back, holding her against the counter. She unbuckled her belt and flipped the tails of the jacket neatly to the side before bending forward. The heavy wool trousers slid towards the floor.

"Mary, I can't do this now. It feels all wrong. Let's just get back to work," I said, as I started to turn away.

Mary reached back behind herself and caught my arm, the force of her grip steely through the latex. As she looked back over her shoulder, the fierceness of her gaze scared me. Just then, Nana appeared in my imagination yet again, bringing the memory of how she would hold her white gloved hands before her and then pull smartly at their edges, tightening them down against the base of her fingers, and how, when she did so, a little funny smile would cross her face.

Mary nodded at me, indicating it was my turn, and I mimicked Nana's gesture, pulling on the long pink sleeves. The tension condensed my fingers into a pointed unit and chased a quick smile across my lips, as well. As I teetered on the edge of decision, the weight of the gloves on my arms comforted me, their heaviness making each move slower and more conscious than usual, their barrier leaving me feeling oddly safe.

"Do it for me," Mary pleaded again, her voice frighteningly far away.

Tentatively, I pushed my foot against hers, spreading her legs further apart. With one hand, I reached into her crotch from behind, scrubbing my fingers through her pubic hair. I could feel the latex catch and pull through the gloves, but I didn't care. Mary moaned as I pressed the palm of my hand deep into the floor of her pelvis, feeling the muscles surrounding her vagina and perineum push back, meeting me through the distance of the gloves. Rather than responding to her body's demands, I flipped my hand over and gave a quick backhanded punch, scolding her naked desire. She spread her legs even wider in response.

I leaned into Mary and placed one hand on the small of her back to hold her in place. She wriggled back against me.

"Not yet," I commanded, slapping her lightly. "This is my kitchen, my rules." As I spoke these words, I could feel their truth. The room became a familiar stage on which the gloves belonged. I reached over and dipped my right hand into the *Crisco*, feeling its thickness give way. I could feel the solid break and slide against my fingers, the cool weight surround my hand, yet I felt it all at a distance. The only thing permeating the gloves was the strange vibration that had been there from the start.

With a slight sucking sound, I pulled my hand from the tin and worked the malleable solid all over the glove's pink surface. The friction created a slippery warmth. My arm started to sweat, and the fabric interior stuck to my skin. I held the lubricated hand up in the air like a surgeon immediately post-scrub and slid the other hand from the small of Mary's back around to the front of her belly, pulling her towards me. I bent forward slightly in order to reach that hand further down to play with her clit. Her hips began to rock, and I saw small beads of sweat gathering on the tiny hairs at the base of her spine. For a moment, I felt like a bare-back rider, one hand exalting towards the sky while reveling in a fleeting moment of dominance over the forces of nature.

Drawing my left hand back around, I drew one finger down through the narrowing V where back transmuted into glutes all the way until my finger found her asshole. I pressed gently, measuring her desire through the pulse at her root, feeling it all through the remote sensation of the *Playtex* glove. I knew Mary loved this kind of play, but I still felt far removed, like I was kissing my lover's photograph.

Another shiver ran though my body, rattling the petals on the upheld glove, pushing me forward.

Moving my left hand back around to her belly, I finally brought the *Crisco*-laden one down and navigated the same trail through her glutes, leaving a slippery trail as I bypassed her anus and headed straight for her pussy.

"I'm afraid it's stuffing time," I stated coolly, warning Mary what was to come. I could feel her vaginal opening clench involuntarily in response to my words and inquiring fingers. As I continued to press, coaxing gently, I could feel the vibration in the gloves increase and start to penetrate her as well. The muscles surrendered, and she slid her hips back towards me, hungry for more. Nana appeared in my peripheral imagination, her head down slightly but smiling as she drifted by, holding a bowl of creamed onions. A wave of longing swept over me, and my knees buckled.

Moving my left hand to the small of Mary's back, I braced myself and squatted down to get a better angle of attack with my right. One of Mary's hands reached back, searching for contact. I slapped it away. Instead, she slid one leg back enough that I could straddle it, my apron-covered crotch spreading against her calf. I allowed her this.

My *Crisco*-coated, *Playtex*-wrapped fingers took one long, slow detour up and around her clit, circling three times before coming back to her cunt. I knew this terrain intimately, knew each curve and fold of Mary like it was my own, knew the tangy wetness that was mixing with the *Crisco* even now . . . and yet, through the glove, it felt unreal. Anger began to rise in me unbidden, as if the gloves infected me with this sense of distance, their pinkness a caustic agent on my heart.

Like a series of curtains, I pushed through Mary's opening. The coarse, spongy, just-inside tissue greeted me, granting me rights of entry like a benign nightclub bouncer. I pushed deeper, the *Crisco* and the *Playtex* making me bold. My hand strutted forward, tips of fingers gliding past the round knob of her cervix , knuckles too, until the base of my palm finally made its dramatic entrance. My whole hand now inside. My fluted wrist vibrated as the deep, dark warmth of Mary held me firm.

I could feel the heat rise in us both—and I resented it. Everything in me told me to pull back, but Mary's strong muscles refused. I felt as if something was pushing me down hard onto her calf. Mary pulsed and rocked, her motions pulling me deeper inside, her calf demanding my own clit to respond. The glitter on the front of the apron scraped across Mary's bare calves, carving deep red welts, but I didn't care. I just wanted this to be over, I wanted to come, I wanted to fuck her, I wanted . . . a jumble of things I couldn't name. My head screamed run, but something else was in charge. I felt hands on my shoulders, forcing me down even harder, forcing me to surrender to all the sensations that radiated through my body, through the gloves, through my heart.

I came fast and hard with Mary in fast succession. As the contractions subsided, I had the distinct feeling again of hands sweetly squeezing my shoulders. I lifted my head and looked forward toward the cabinets. They shape-shifted into the old three-fold mirror and I saw Nana's reflection as she stood behind me, her hands resting on my shoulders, a gentle smile on her lips as her love flooded over me.

Whatever had been locked inside me finally broke free. I leaned my face into Mary's thighs, wrapping both pink *Playtex* hands around her tightly. She quietly reached down and stroked my hair as I sobbed . . . for the love that fills us up and all the losses that make us whole.

No matter what time of year you're reading them, this next suite of poems from Rose Mark will evoke the sweet juiciness of hot summer afternoons. Mmmm-hmmm.

Rose K. Mark

THE SUMMER OF RIPE PEACHES

The peaches have passed their prime,

The season has now ended,

My tongue

no longer

can taste

you

Autumn arrives tomorrow

Winter to follow.

Rose K. Mark

ODE TO A FRESH BLACK MISSION FIG

Black beauty
I behold you.
Dark purple globes,
I hold your teardrop offering
In the palm of my hand.

Your velvety skin,
Asks to be stroked
Nibbled.

I spread you apart.

My lips are
Nervous
Seeing your
Pink, tender, moist
Flesh

What will happen
When my tongue
Touches those first succulent
Waving tendrils ?

I fear

There will be an explosion,
A gushing
Of delight

Of which
I will be too embarrassed to
Show in public.

Rose K. Mark

ODE TO AN O'HENRY PEACH

I've been waiting this long hot summer for you,
Others have touched my lips,
Crisp, delicate, virginal, fragrant
But none has stirred my juices
Like you.

O'Henry,
Let me bite you
Caress your fullness
Between
My lips and tongue,
Suck every juicy morsel
Of your being
And swallow

O'Henry,
Come to me
Fill me with your succulence,
Let your nectar
Drool over my lips,
Run down my chin

O'Henry,
I can't get enough of you

Come to me

Again and again and again

O... Henry!

I'm an organic gardener and a beekeeper. These activities are a welcome balance to the cerebral activity of writing. The garden and the beehive feel like essential extensions of my femininity, and they give me the same intense sensual pleasure as I get from stroking my mate's skin. It's even better if I can combine the two, as I do in this – unfortunately fictional – story.

IN THE GARDEN

I've always been a creative dabbler. In the 1970s, I
was a potter. In the 80s, I did performance art. I've made
sculptures out of found objects and done large-scale
paintings. The problem with painting and sculpture,
though, is that you make them and then ... there they are,
cluttering things up. So now, I garden.

A garden is a work of art that unfolds over time.
Every day is new, and there's no end to it. Leaves fall,
blossoms burst, creatures devour, I protect. Life and
death, and I'm the goddess – even if my power over the life
of the garden is weaker than Mother Nature's.

My garden is like a lover, filling my hands and
mouth – the best kind of lover, one who always changes
but would never leave me. My garden won't get run down
and flabby and tired, and then run off with one of his
students in a ridiculous attempt to bring back his youth.

I hadn't had actual sex in several years. Harry and
I had fallen into a drought even before he left me for
Monica, a girl so young and shapeless that I couldn't even
hate her for breaking up my marriage. I'd been keeping
half an eye open for an opportunity, but most of my

attention was on the pulse of my daily life. More and more of that revolved around the garden.

This day was pure California April, the season when life and death collide in the dirt. The afternoon was moist and sweet with sun. I had my mental checklist for this session: weed out the lettuce bed and get the rest of the carrots out of the ground. I'd overplanted the carrots. Those tiny seeds had drifted out of my hands on the breeze and turned into carrot after carrot after carrot. I'd been selectively pulling them all winter, seeing them come out thicker and longer.

I had so many carrots that I'd put out a call on our local Crop Swap email list, inviting people to give me a hand and take home some of the bounty. I'd only gotten one bite, so to speak. A guy named Pete was coming by, with a bottle of home-made mead to pay me back for the veggies.

I'd just finished clearing the lettuce bed when he showed up. I'd been expecting one of the hipsters who've been colonizing my North Oakland neighborhood – sweet kids into kombucha-making and backyard chickens. But Pete was my age or maybe even older. His hair was a gorgeous, tousled white that gave back the sun in sparkles, and he had a short beard that was equally luminous.

I stood up, stripped off a glove and held out my hand. "Hi, Pete. I'm Nina."

He had a strong hand and a strong, thick arm to wield it. His eyes were bright blue, and his face was ruddy with outdoors. There was nothing remotely Santa Claus about him.

"What a beautiful garden," he said.

"Thank you." He knew how to wield words, too, to win a gardener's heart.

He fingered the skin of a Hand of Buddha, the citrus fruit that looks more like an octopus. "This is amazing." He bent to it and let its scent expand his chest. His body was still lithe and flexible, I noticed. "Ahh," he said.

"Take one home." I pulled my pruning shears out of my back pocket and snipped the stem of the one with the plumpest, juiciest tendrils, handed it to him. I couldn't stop looking at his hands. I pulled my eyes away. "So. Carrots?"

He smiled. "Let's do it."

"Why don't you start at this end, and I'll work in from the other end?" We'd meet in the middle.

"Sounds like a plan."

He knelt at the edge of the bed, rummaged through his canvas bag and pulled out a hori hori. My respect for him went up a notch. The hori hori is like a bayonet, only better; it's a serious gardening tool. I went to the far side of the bed, knelt on my knee pads and pulled my own hori hori out of the leg pocket of my pants. I held it up in a toast to him. "Happy digging."

The earth was hot, moist and soft. Carrots gave up their grip and slid out of the soil. I fell into a rhythm. Grip the fuzzy top with my left hand, use my shoulder to drive the hori hori deep alongside the carrot's body, a quick levering motion with the tool and then pull with my left hand. April breeze blew lavender at us; birds swooped in to peck at the turned-up dirt in the lettuce patch, keeping a wary eye on the two human intruders. I'd look over at Pete every once in a while, watching him get closer. As often as not, he'd feel my eyes on him and look back at me.

We were on the last few feet of the carrot patch, just an arm's length away from each other, when I unearthed the mother of all carrots. Or, I should say, the father. It was almost as thick as my wrist, meaty and vigorous, with a bulge at the top that narrowed down to a blunt tip some seven inches later.

I held it up. "Whoah. Look at this monster."

He laughed. "Don't wave that thing at me. It looks dangerous."

Still holding it up, I brushed the dirt off it, at first with my fingertips and then, what the heck, sliding my palm along it.

I'm not above having sex with my vegetables once in a while. Why not? They're fresh and organic, unlike Harry. A carrot may not be as effective as my vibrator, but sometimes they come up with an interesting knob or two that I can't resist. And there's something so suggestive about a zucchini. I've watched a zucchini swell, day after day, until its heft felt just right for my pussy.

So, stroking this carrot, I was suggesting. Then, as I kept stroking and he kept smiling and didn't look away, I was asking. He was a courteous man, though, not presuming even as my own smile made the invitation clearer. He'd let me make the first move, just to be sure.

It was so easy. I was sitting back on my heels, carrot in hand. All I had to do was rise up on my knees and then lean forward, planting my hands inches from his knees. I smelled him: bitter odor of salt on his skin and the deeper, hormone-infused aroma from his armpits, all of it sweetened with the smell of the fresh air. He put one hand on my waist, tentatively, as much to steady me as to feel me. I tasted him, put my tongue on the delicate skin in front of his ear: salty. I moved my tongue to lightly flick the little protrusion that guards the ear canal. A moan came from deep in his throat, getting louder as I thrust my tongue deeper. I fell against his chest and his arms came around me. We were doing this.

My mouth was already open and ready when we kissed. When his tongue filled it, my belly opened with heat. My pussy buzzed like the yellow jackets in the flowers around us. When we pulled away and looked into each other's eyes, I was gasping. It had been so long that I was instantly ignited.

Pete looked around. My garden is relatively screened by the fruit trees around the edges, but you can see neighbors' windows. "Do you want to go inside?" he asked.

I hesitated. I didn't. It had been close to a year since Harry had left, but suddenly the inside of the house seemed to still reek of him. I unbuttoned a couple buttons on my shirt and pulled it over my head. The sun on my bare breasts made me hotter. "It's okay. No one can see," I lied.

He put his hands on my breasts, cupping and squeezing them, then bent his lips to a nipple. My god. I felt like they'd never been touched before. I twisted my legs over his lap, and he laid me down on my back, still licking and squeezing.

I used to worship the sun. He paid me back for my devotion by branding me with freckles, so now I approach the garden all bundled up. While I love and appreciate my dirt, my relationship with it is usually removed. It was a shock to feel it on my bare back, and at first, I shied away from the feeling. Tickly clumps of dirt and bits of carrot top on my back; warm, hard Pete on my front. Then I gave myself to the dirt and to him.

Desire like a million ants crawled over my body. The sun drenched me with honey. In the garden, where you're down in the essentials of life, even clichés become true again. My pussy was a ripe peach waiting to be split open. I was juicy.

I ran my hands under his t-shirt. His body was firm and damp with his own heat. He reared up long enough to strip off his shirt and then buried his face in my neck. The bristle of his beard against my tender skin sent an ache all the way down to my clit. His hands slid under me and grasped my butt, pulling my crotch against his hard cock.

I wanted those hands on my pussy. But I knew the garden grit would grate. I wanted his cock in my pussy, but that wasn't going to happen, I decided.

I took his right hand, brought it to my mouth and sucked. I sucked each strong finger in turn, running my tongue from the tender place at its root up to the fingernail, working it around the nail to clean it, and then taking the whole thing in my mouth. I was getting a mouthful of dirt, but filling my mouth with his fingers was every bit as good as sucking cock had ever been.

Pete undid my pants and slid them down to my knees; there'd be no getting them off over my work boots. Then he undid his own jeans and pulled his shorts down to free his cock. He used his cleaned-up hand to rub my pussy lips and clit through my panties. They were wet through. I was moaning and gasping, needing more. He pulled my panties down and spread my lips to make my clit pop up out of its hood. I pulled his hand back up to my mouth to make his fingers really wet, then he slid two inside me while his thumb massaged my clit. I was writhing, digging myself down into the rich earth like a bursting seed.

I quickly licked my own fingers clean. Why had I never appreciated how good soil could taste, how the grit between my teeth could be like the grit of life? I took his cock in my wet fingers and gripped the base, feeling its heat and firmness. I slid my hand up the shaft, running my fingers along the head, finding a bit of precum, spreading it, taking in the smoothness of the skin on the head, the rougher, slightly stretchy skin of the shaft.

The palm of my hand and the walls of my pussy clamping around Pete's fingers were one thing. My entire body was connected to itself, to Pete and, through the dirt, it seemed, to the whole earth. I came so hard I squeezed his fingers out of my pussy. He went to put them back in, but I stayed his hand and placed it over my mound.

"Just hold me there."

Letting my pussy relax into his warm grip, I changed my focus to how I was making him feel. His cock was pulsing, and his balls were tight. He was close. He rolled over onto his side, propping himself up on the hand that wasn't on my pussy, so I could get better access. I let my strokes get more even, paced them, slow, fast, slow, fast. And I swear I felt it when it started in his balls, his come shooting up and out, over my hand, onto my chest, onto his lap. The smell of it was the smell of a root vegetable cut open right after it sprang out of the dirt.

When the rhythm of my hand seemed to be too much, I took it away, licked my fingers to taste this part of him. He lay back on top of me, his own body basted with soil and sweat. I was replete.

The future might bring a tentative twining with Pete or maybe a retreat from something too entangling. But today, we had honored spring and fertilized the garden.

Her pudenda have an agenda? I can't top that, so you'll just have to enjoy this next poem by Selene Steese without further introduction.

Selene Stccoo

GODDESS IN MY PANTS

My pussy throws wide the gates
of her pink, perfect, glistening palace.
She has got something to say.

My pudenda's got an agenda.
My twat wants to talk,
to have a cunt-versation.

My vulva voices, "Touch me more.
When you're alone,
reach into your pants
and hold me. Remind me you love me.
Let me know you remember
I am here."

My nether mouth tells me, "Eat less salt.
It dries me out. Your body
is a temple, and I am the Goddess
you should worship there."

The sweet, wet, furry Goddess
in my pants says, "When you pleasure
yourself, invite the whole family:

The Labia sisters,
Majora and Minora!
Doris the Clitoris,
that excitable, wild thing!
Gina the G-Spot, who's always elusive—
but you sure can have fun looking!"

My pudenda reminds me, "Laugh more.
And I don't mean breathy
chest giggles; I mean rolling on the floor
laughing, helpless with hilarity laughing—
big, bad belly laugh laughing!"

My cunt tells me, "Surrender
to your own beauty. You don't need to be
rude, crude, or nude to exude
miles and miles of yoni-tude.

If you have trouble believing I am beautiful,
wake up early one morning
and watch the sun rise. Look at all that
luscious deep rosy pink as it fills the sky.

Find and cup the fleshy moistness of a calla lily
between your two hands.

Hold a slick, smooth cowry shell
cradled in your palm.

Slice open a fresh fig and gaze
at all that pink, sweet, sticky perfection

And ask yourself, 'How am I less beautiful'?"

When I heard Resurrección read this at the Octopus Literary Salon, I knew I wanted it for this anthology. She asked me, "Do you think it's appropriate?" My answer was, "Heck yes." This weird retelling of a Mexican folk tale has it all: spooky Gothic atmosphere, sublime eroticism, and transgressive religious imagery, all topped with a dollop of horror. It's the only piece in this book that isn't specifically about an older woman, but it's clearly the work of a mature writer at the height of her powers.

Resurrección is the author of *Santora: The Good Daughter*, a miraculously blasphemous novel about a sexy healer who becomes an unwilling saint of the barrio.

A MARTYR FOR ST. AGNES

One hundred fifty years ago, when the city of Mexico was still a small pueblo with dirt roads, there was a Spanish adobe church on what was then the outskirts of town. Priests lived in a rectory behind the church, and a convent for nuns stood on the other side of a garden courtyard. This church was dedicated to the virgin martyr St. Agnes, a statue of whom stood on one side of the altar near heavy wooden side doors. The statue was vivid in its portrayal of the saint: a beautiful girl with lilies on her painted robes, holding a lamb and a palm frond in one arm, and an unsheathed Spanish sword in the other. In Catholic art, martyrs are frequently portrayed with the symbols of their martyrdom, and Agnes had been beheaded by the Romans for daring to dedicate her virginity to the Christian God.

One late afternoon in early spring, a terrible storm blew in and raged over the city. Father Juan de la Cruz, the youngest of the priests, lit candles, preparing the church for confession. Usually old Father Caldero heard confession on Saturday nights, but he had taken ill, and Father Juan had elected to take his place.

Although he doubted anyone would venture out on a night like this, he kissed his sacred stole and put it on before entering the confessional. There he held his lonely vigil in darkness, praying while the storm raged outside.

Someone opened the penitents' door of the confessional, entered and knelt at the window. Father Juan slid open the little wooden door between them and leaned toward the latticed privacy screen.

"Bless me Father, for I have sinned," came the sweet voice of a woman. "It has been seven days since my last confession."

Glancing through the latticed screen, he could just make out the white robes of a religious habit, the black veil shadowing her face. It was one of the nuns from the convent. What lay so heavily on her conscience that she would come out on such a night? But all that followed were the usual sins of nuns: those of gossip, envy, and disobedience. Then she stopped, saying nothing for a long time.

"Yes, my child, is there something else?" he finally prompted.

"Father...I am guilty of a terrible sin."

Ah, upon occasion he had experienced this as well: shame-filled hesitation, usually due to sins of self-pollution.

"Is it the sin of vice, my daughter?"

"No—um, yes, I don't know. I..." Suddenly the nun broke down, weeping.

"Father, I don't know what to do. I have prayed over this, I've taken on extra work, scrubbing all the floors of the convent, trying to distract myself. I cannot sleep. I wake in a sweat from terrible dreams. I whip my naked back and thighs with my rosary, but nothing distracts me from this evil fire. The object of temptation is so frequently before me, I don't know what to do. Please, help me."

"And the sin, my child? What is it you've done?"

"I have—oh God—I am in love."

This too he had heard: nuns who had given into the temptation of that perversion between women that could never yield children, and so was a sin of pure lust. By now he had recognized the voice: Sor Magdalena, the youngest nun at St. Agnes. She was very beautiful, with large sad eyes, pure skin, and a lovely, soft mouth. She couldn't have been more than nineteen. Who, whether man or woman, wouldn't have been tempted by such a face?

"I understand. And does she return your love?" He heard a quick intake of breath.

"*She?* Father, what are you talking about? I am a woman, and a nun! It is a *man* I'm in love with!"

In a rush, she told him the story of what she believed was her perfect vocation, entering the convent against her parents' wishes, how she would not listen when they said she was too young to know her heart. About being a model novice, obedient, submissive, and infinitely devout. And how shortly after taking her final vows, all her certainty and resolve had disintegrated when a new priest arrived at St. Agnes.

"He is young and beautiful," she said. "He plays the guitar and has a beautiful singing voice. He is kind, and wise, and so good! When he first came to St. Agnes's a year ago—"

Why, she is speaking of me! thought Father Juan.

"I couldn't take my eyes off him when he was near. If I was outside, I found myself constantly looking for him. I realized I wanted him, in the way a woman wants her husband in the marital bed. I knew it was wrong. I believed God was testing me.

"So I began avoiding occasions of sin. If I saw him, I turned away. In mass, I kept my eyes down the whole time. When he came into my thoughts, I filled my mind with prayer. For a while I believed my temptation conquered.

"Then one night, I had a blasphemous dream. All was darkness. I was on a cross, suffering as our Divine Savior did. I was...I was...I was completely unclothed. Then *he* came out of the darkness, took down the cross with me still writhing upon it. He soothed me so kindly, stroking me gently, releasing me from my torment.

"Suddenly his tender concern turned into fiendish ravishment. Too late I realized it was not my priest at all, but the devil, wearing the guise of my good priest to approach me. He threw himself on top of me and forced his long tongue into my mouth. He licked me, first my wounds, then my whole body and even—put the vile thing into my secret parts! At first I struggled, but he ordered me to submit to him, and—and God save me—when I did, I became unresistingly wanton, kissing him back, my tongue playing with his. I even grasped him with my arms and legs, refusing to let go of him. *The very devil himself!*"

She had never given Father Juan the slightest indication of her attraction. Not a word or glance. He had noticed she stopped taking communion; guessed she suffered from some terrible spiritual affliction; had prayed for her. Never had he imagined it was about this passion.

"Since then, I have known no peace. I know that dream was my punishment for the sin of pride, for imagining that I, above all, had what it took to be a nun. I even believed I had the makings of a saint. But my continuing dreams have taught me it was all nothing but fanaticism and sanctimonious hubris! Father, why has God chosen *this* to show me the error of my ways?"

But she didn't wait for an answer.

"Since then, I have not been able to put aside the love I feel for my priest. On the days he says mass, I dare not receive communion from his hands. I fear I will not be able to control myself, that I will—I will pull him down on top of me, there in front of Our Lord and everyone, and force him to make love with me as the devil does, every night! Help me, Father. Tell me what to do."

Sor Magdalena wept as she continued her confession.

"That isn't all. I...I intentionally cultivate fantasies of him. I imagine that he comes to my cell in the middle of the night and forces me to perform sacrilegious love acts upon him, as he then does upon me.

"All the nuns hear my screams and know what is happening. Only they are not screams of terror and agony, but those of base, sensual pleasure. I bite him, wanting to consume every part of him. I suck him, and I drink not only his precious and sacred fluid of procreation, but I suck his blood like a fiend, and I feel transformed, as I used to, after partaking of the holy bread and wine.

"Then I am dragged before the inquisition. In the candlelit room of judgment, my beautiful priest grabs the veil from my head, pulls my hair until it becomes undone, then strips off my habit until I am standing naked and cold, my nipples shamelessly growing and hardening for all to see. He orders me to confess all my dreams to the holy men and judges. I do, only I feel no proper shame! I giggle and laugh with joy and derision at their holy office.

"Then my priest lifts me in his arms and carries me to the torturer's table, where he uses chains and ropes to fasten me. He blindfolds me, then with one, maddening finger, he slowly touches me everywhere, even inside my ears, my mouth, even that foul organ used to expel waste—after which he smells that finger. And lastly, he carefully spreads my nether lips, and touches and rubs every part of it, taking care to enter my very darkness in his search for the witches' marks that will prove my evil! My breath becomes shallow and labored and concentrated, and then suddenly, before all those men, my body rocks with unbelievable ecstasy, and my priest's hand is doused with my shameful fluid."

Despite the cold, Father Juan had begun to sweat. Should he go on pretending he was not hearing her profess her love for him, or should he reveal himself–and admit his love for her?

"I feel sometimes that I can no longer live without him. Is it my cross to find a way to conquer it? Or is this suffering something I must endure? Father, advise me, and I will do it."

He could stand it no longer. Forgetting his vows, ignoring the occasion of sin which was upon him, he pushed aside the lattice door and said, "Sor Magdalena, it is I."

The nun gasped and covered her mouth with her hands. "Oh my God—" She stumbled up, about to run away, but he reached out and grasped her hand.

"Stay," he begged. "For I, too, have struggled with my conscience. I have thought endlessly of you. I never thought—never realized you might return my love."

"But, now you know all my horrible secrets—"

"Never mind," he said, drawing her hand to his lips and soothing her. She was like a young, frightened doe, ready to bolt at any moment. At last, he drew her towards him and kissed her lips, and they were softer and warmer than he had ever imagined. She gasped when his tongue entered her mouth, though unlike his dream counterpart, he was gentle, slowly sucking her tongue into his own mouth, imagining what it would be like to suck her soft nipples and feel them harden between his lips, doing the same with her wet and virginal lower lips, taking them in like a sun-warmed, luscious apricot. Sor Magdalena's shock soon turned to sensuous response, not unlike what she had described in her dreams.

But then she pulled away.

"Father, this love is impossible, and to indulge ourselves is sinful. Now that you know all my shame, I cannot continue to live so close to you. Rather than expose ourselves to further temptation and sin, I will leave the convent and never see you again."

But Father Juan could not bear the thought of having no more of this bliss. He said, "Then I will go with you. We will go someplace far away, where no one knows we were once religious. We will start over and make our vows to each other before God alone. We will live together as man and wife. Surely He can understand a love like ours, He who *is* love, who created love, and will forgive us? Will you do this?"

Though weeping once again, she at last agreed.

"Let us go tonight, under cover of storm. No one will know we are missing until morning, and the storm will cover our tracks. Go back to the convent, find some women's clothes in the poor box, and put those on. Pack whatever you wish to take, for we will never return. Then meet me back here.

"Leave now, but before you return to the convent,

stop by the altar and pray as if you are saying your penance. We must behave as usual, in case anyone else is about. I will wait in here another half hour. Now go."

After kissing each other once more and professing their love, Sor Magdalena left the confessional. She went up to the altar as her beloved had instructed, genuflected, then went to kneel before the statue of St. Agnes.

Unbeknownst to Father Juan, Sor Magdalena was still battling with her conscience. She had hoped the old priest would know how to counsel her, would bring her some relief. Instead, she had revealed all to the very priest over whom she had been struggling with temptation for months. Was not what he had urged her to do more sin? The trouble was, she *wanted* to do what he suggested.

Oh dear St. Agnes, is this the right thing to do? She prayed. *What is the greater sin? Please, give me a sign!*

It was time for Sor Magdalena to leave the church. The storm seemed even worse than before, howling like a thousand devils riding the wind. Sor Magdalena stood up and moved the few feet to the side entrance, but when she opened the heavy doors, a huge gust of wind blew them out of her hands, throwing them wide open. Great gusts of rain, leaves and branches blew in, drenching her instantly, pushing her back and even tearing her veil partway off. She paused to take it and the wimple off.

I'll never wear it again anyway, she thought sadly.

Just as she was about to head into the raging wind, the statue of St. Agnes rocked on its pedestal. Sor

Magdalena reflexively turned toward the statue, arms raised to steady the saint, but it was already tumbling, slowly falling toward her. As she stood transfixed, staring into the castigating eyes of the saint, it seemed Agnes was brandishing the sword. As the statue toppled, the sword sliced cleanly through her neck. Sor Magdalena's body crumpled where she stood, her head rolling several feet into the aisle.

Father Juan, hearing the commotion, left the confessional and walked down the side aisle toward the open doors and roaring wind.

Magdalena must not have been able to close the doors, he thought.

Something rolled to his feet and stopped, staring up at him with the wide, quickly dulling eyes of his beloved. Father Juan fell to his knees.

My God, what have we done?

Even in the midst of abject grief, he knew this was God's way of preventing them from committing the terrible sins they had planned—*no,* he alone, Juan de la Cruz, failed priest, had thought up and thrust upon the innocent young nun. His lust had blinded him, caused him to nearly break his vows and encourage another to sin. Now the beautiful Sor Magdalena was dead. Worst of all, she had come to him for absolution and had not received it before dying. Now she would suffer for centuries in the lonely fires of purgatory.

Maddened by grief, Father Juan picked up her

head, and with his fingers, closed the beautiful, empty eyes forever. He wrapped the head in her veil and fled into the night.

The storm ended just before dawn. That's when the headless body was discovered, and Father Juan found to be missing. The police were summoned. After asking questions and studying the evidence, the chief of police went to the abbot and abbess to report their findings.

"The nun was in the church last night, probably for confession. When she tried to leave, the wind from the storm no doubt blew in, causing the statue to fall and cut off her head with the unsheathed sword—a freak accident. The priest, hearing the commotion of the banging doors, perhaps even a scream, came out of the confessional—the door was hanging open and his stole left behind—found the young nun had been killed.

"The reason for his disappearance is unexplained; Father Juan left no note. Perhaps he somehow felt responsible for the young nun's death. Perhaps he became unhinged by the horrible sight, and he wandered off, taking her head with him. I have my officers searching the city for a priest carrying a woman's head."

Father Juan was never found, and Sor Magdalena was buried without her head. They say that her ghost still haunts the ancient church. Every year, on the anniversary of her death, the nun has been sighted, headless, drifting aimlessly around the church as if searching for her head.

Far away, a broken man worked as the sexton of a small, coastal mission. He spoke little and never revealed that he was an ordained priest. In addition to digging graves, cleaning the church, and ringing the mission bell, he took care of the garden. He was particularly protective of a small lemon tree he had planted in a pot at the back of the cemetery. All he would say about it was that he'd chosen a lemon tree because its fruit is bitter.

I'm ending this collection with a poem by Selene Steese that's a call to arms— as well as to hands, fingers, toys and flesh.

Selene Steese

I WANT TO STOP MASTURBATING

No more furtively fingering
the fur pie at five in the afternoon,
wondering, "Can the neighbors
hear me when I come?"

No more worrying if I'm addicted
to the vibrator, if it's a bad sign
that I hear that hive-of-bees
sound and my cunt
(no, I hate that word)
my vagina
(way too damn clinical)
my crotch
(what the hell am I, a tree?)
my nether mouth
that wonderful
warm, furry place
between my thighs,
gets juiced up, slicked
and slippery, ready for that divine
sliding ride.

I want to stop masturbating.
Stop making that act a dark corners

part of my life and transform it
into a sacred act of self love.

I'm going to get out the massage oil
and rub it lovingly over
my ear lobes, the nape
of my neck, the bony points
of elbow, my spinal ridge.

I'm going to strum myself
like a fine old cello—discover
just what sounds this aging,
mellow flesh can make. I'll
worship at my own feet—
work my way up my ankles,
slowly slide one finger along
my shin bone, spider
the other hand across my
shapely calves.

I'll caress my beautiful
knees, linger on the stubble
of those little hairs I can never
quite reach with the razor.

Say hello, old friends,
to my thighs.

I'll bypass my nether mouth,
move to my belly and appreciate
the total non-
conformity to what the magazines
call beautiful. I will love every inch
of that flesh because it is me.
Just as my choices are me, just
as my ambitions are me. My dreams
define this self no less than does
this yielding, downy flesh.

I will appreciate me from the top
of my curly thatch to my ribcage
just below my breasts. I will bypass
my breasts, explore shoulders,
clavicles, find the shapes
of flesh-and-skin-wrapped bones,
get high on the soft-yet-solid
feel of me.

I'll stop there. I just remembered
that I have an urgent and pressing
engagement. Bye for now—
and don't do anything I wouldn't do.

More about the authors

Amy Butcher is a writer, illustrator, and silver fox "liminal guide" who enjoys leading people through transformation. She is the author the 2012 award-winning mystery novel, *Paws for Consideration*. Her latest project is the soon-to-be-released adult coloring book, *Wonder Body*. Learn more at AmyButcher.com.

Lynx Canon loves to mash up erotica with other genres. She's the author of the *Alien Captive Series*, available on Amazon, and the organizer and host of the Dirty Old Women reading series at Oakland's Octopus Café. Her alter ego is a technology and business journalist. Find out more at LynxCanon.com.

Resurrección Cruz is a writer and storyteller who has collected Mexican folktales for over twenty years. She is the author of *Santora, The Good Daughter*, a Latina novel. She has been published by Penthouse and has written columns titled *The Coconut Chronicles* and *La Post-Modern Curandera* for *The New Mission News* in San Francisco. She has degrees in literature, art, women's spirituality, and library and information science. She works as a librarian and lives in Oakland with her partner and their two bad cats. Resurrección Cruz is a pseudonym.

Beth Elliott has a background in magazines and a weekly newspaper as a reviewer and columnist. She has had a novel and a biography published. The two stories in this anthology are from an as-yet-unpublished collection of experimental erotic fiction, *The Smart Drug Masochists and Other Stories*.

Stella Fosse is a sixty-something SF Bay Area technical writer who came alive sexually in her late fifties. She writes about the joys and absurdities of arriving at the party just when other folks are packing up to go home. Stella enjoys gathering with other similarly situated women to write and laugh together. Find her at StellaFosse.com.

Dorothy Freed is a mature Bay Area erotica writer. Her stories appear in anthologies including: *Best Women's Erotica of the Year, Vol. 1, Dirty Dates: Erotic Fantasies For Couples, For The Men: And The Women Who Love Them, Sex Still Spoken Here, Ageless Erotica,* and *Cheeky Spanking Stories*. Her website is DorothyFreedWrites.com.

Rose K. Mark is a sensualist. Her poems and stories share the sensual allure and pleasure of everyday objects and interactions. Her book, *Tasting Life,* a collection of stories, poems and recipes about her favorite subject, *FOOD,* can be purchased from Amazon.

Kristin McCloy is a novelist with three books published (*Velocity*, Random House; *Some Girls*, Viking/Penguin, and *Hollywood Savage*, Atria Books, Simon & Schuster) and a fourth on its very painful way. She has also published short stories and book reviews, as well as taught a fiction workshop, which she would be most happy to re-start, given students' interest. You can find her at KristinMcCloy.Blogspot.com.

J Mork is a longtime resident of San Francisco. J has written and performed in the Bay Area focusing around issues of disability and sexuality. J loves to travel and has an ability to make any hotel an erotic wonderland or a writing retreat.

Chris Orr is a writer, cybrarian and bicyclist who lives right smack on the Oakland-Berkeley line where she is inspired by the dual nature of existence as material and spirit.

Anita Placebo's dreams come true. She delights in nature, the smell of your body and your loving touch. She is a dedicated student of Human Relationship, Body Language and Metaphysics.

Jan Steckel's book *The Horizontal Poet* (Zeitgeist Press, 2011) won a 2012 Lambda Literary Award. Her chapbooks *Mixing Tracks* (Gertrude Press, 2009) and *The Underwater*

Hospital (Zeitgeist Press, 2006) also won awards. Her writing has appeared in *Scholastic Magazine, Yale Medicine, Bellevue Literary Review,* and elsewhere. Visit her at JanSteckel.com.

Selene Steese credits writing with saving her life. "I felt very lonely growing up," she says. "Words gave me focus, provided a lens through which I could make sense of the world." Reflecting on her song *Addicted to Words*, she says, "I can't imagine a healthier or more life-affirming addiction than my obsession with committing poetry."

Donna George Storey is the author of *Amorous Woman,* an erotic novel based on her experiences living in Japan. Her stories have appeared in over 150 other publications including *Penthouse* and *Best American Erotica.* She is also a monthly columnist for the Erotica Readers and Writers blog. Her home on the web is DonnaGeorgeStorey.com.

Made in the USA
San Bernardino, CA
12 August 2017